Why Some Cats are Rascals

Book 3

Boszenna Nowiki

Healthy Life Press Inc.

Published by:
Healthy Life Press Inc.
1685 H Street PMB 860
Blaine,Wa 98230 USA
Tel. 1 (888) 575-3173
info@StartHealthyLife.com

www.StartHealthyLife.com

First Edition

ISBN-10: 0-9727328-6-1
ISBN-13: 978-0-9727328-6-4

LCCN 2006935496

Printed in Canada

The book is dedicated to all cats, cat-lovers and caring veterinarians from CATANADA and the rest of the world.

Although the story is fiction, many of the historical and geographic references such as The Oregon Trail and Sequoyah Alphabet, are real. Just as real are the characters of the book. They live with me in a white wooden house with a big garden and a magnificent view of mountains. Their names are real too, but some of them, like Grandma Calico and Uncle Toothless, are now on the other side of the rainbow...

The central character, Rascal, is a four year old, orange colored male. He is anything but the typical, cuddly 'lap-cat'. His behavior seems to justify his name, but if the truth be known, his heart is that of an angel. And it shows so clearly while he cares for the kitten Onyx, recently adopted from the SPCA.

I hope this book provides readers with a pleasant escape from everyday concerns, whether related to school or home. If any reader plans using this or any other of my novels in a class setting or book club, please let me know. I'd be delighted to meet with the group and chat about Rascal and other cats. I'd like to hear your thoughts about this or other books of mine, as well as any views which relate to cats, children problems, and life in general.

And, if you are just a plain 'ole' cat lover, perhaps with a cat story to share, feel free to contact me by email at **rascalandfriends@gmail.com**

Boszenna Nowiki
www.catsarerascals.com

Part 1

Wildly Wild West

1

Rascal was sitting on the windowsill, looking sadly out the window. Grandma Calico was gone. She had gone to the other side of the rainbow where all cats go when their time in this life has come to an end. Rascal began writing in his diary. He knew that Grandma was happy and free from disease. Philosopher was reading a book. Lumby did not understand the situation but he could feel the sadness of all the others. He was lying near the window, watching a fly on it taking an autumn sun bath. Sofia was crying in the corner of the room; Dandy was comforting Snow. Bunny was sad too, knowing that he would never again hear all those interesting stories about the old times that Grandma Calico used to tell them.

Philosopher closed his book and made his way over to Rascal. "It might be a good idea for us to take a little walk outside. Help us to get our minds off our sadness. What do you think, brother?"

"I think that's a very good idea, Philosopher. Sofia is not handling Grandma Calico's absence well at all. I think a little adventure might be a good thing today."

So, to give themselves a break from grieving, the cats decided to venture into the forest. Rascal led the way, then Philosopher, with three-month-old Lumby jumping alongside him. Then came Bunny, with Snow and Dandy. Last came Sofia, murmuring something about guilt and shame. After a while they arrived at the entrance of the old mine that they had found on their last journey into the forest. A sign above the entrance announced, "Danger!"

"Hey, Rascal, look and read," pointed Philosopher.

"Don't worry, brother," said Rascal, "it simply means that we can go in and there will be lots of adventure waiting for us ahead. See, it's a Cat Hole! Hmm, maybe we'll find something interesting inside."

It was not the Enchanted Forest, so the cats did not find Prehistoric Cat Samuel, but soon after entering the large, round mine tunnel, Rascal saw a ghost cat. He was ready to go back when the ghost said with a faint voice, "Please help me."

"Who's there?" asked Sofia almost bumping into Rascal.

"It...it...it's a cat," murmured Rascal, looking intently at the transparent image of a cat floating in the air.

"Holy Cat!" said Philosopher, who was just behind Sofia.

"What's that?" asked the other cats.

"Please, help me," said the ghost cat.

"How can we help you?" asked Rascal.

"Come closer, sit down and I'll explain."

The cats sat down. Bunny's eyes were wide open, Snow was trembling, Sofia was praying and Lumby said, "Hi! Why are you so pale? You're almost transparent. You look cool! I want to be a ghost, too."

The ghost cat smiled and said, "A long time ago I was in the flesh like you guys. I had a nice life."

"So, what are you doing here?" asked Dandy.

"I'll tell you. My name is Wandering Sheriff and I helped tame the Wild West. Then I promised to write a book about it because nobody knows how very helpful cats were in taming the Wild West. I said that I would write it tomorrow. But tomorrow was again tomorrow and still I didn't write. Tomorrow never comes, because tomorrow is always tomorrow! Now I'm a ghost but not a writer."

"Don't worry, our Rascal is a writer, but not a ghost. He'll help you for sure. Right, Rascal?" asked Philosopher.

"He never says tomorrow, he does everything right now, never waiting. So far he's written three books, diaries," added Snow.

"That's right, I can even write while I'm sleeping," said Rascal, smiling. But then in a more serious tone, he said to the ghost cat, "Okay, I'll write for you everything you tell me. That way I'll set you free and you can go to the other side of the rainbow bridge, right?"

"When you get there say hello to our Grandma

Calico. She went to the other side of the rainbow too," said Snow.

"I promise!" said the ghost cat.

"I promise, too! I'll write your book. I'll write only the truth, but if I forget the truth I will invent it," said Rascal and looked at Wandering Sheriff for a hint about what to do next.

Wandering Sheriff was quiet for a moment, thinking about how to begin. "I think, the best way is to go back in time. I'll show you the Wild West and how it really was. That way you won't have to invent anything, because you'll be there and you'll feel, smell and see everything with all your senses."

"Yes!" agreed the cats.

With the ghost cat floating in the air, the others followed him through the copper mine, along old corridors and down holes. Rascal noticed that with every minute Wandering Sheriff was more visible and he began to walk, not float. His color was the same orange as Rascal's, but he didn't have dark spots on his nose and he was much bigger and stronger then Rascal.

2

After a few hours of making their way through dusty corridors full of stones, the cats came out into the sunlight. They could see distant snow-covered mountains. Closer still was a small town and they could see humans going about their business. They noticed there were no cars: everyone was going around on horseback. On the outskirts of the town, they could see small farms and houses.

Wandering Sheriff led them to the sheriff's office. The door was open and outside was a black cat, sitting and reading a newspaper. He glanced up and, seeing the group of strangers, he reached for his guns. With a second glance, he recognized Wandering Sheriff, smiled and said, "Howdy, Pardner, and welcome to Cats Valley. It's good to see you looking so well."

"Howdy, Black Crow," said Wandering Sheriff with a smile, then he turned toward Rascal and the other cats and said, "This is my right hand cat. He's very smart...the best town sheriff ever."

They all went inside. Rascal looked around

with curiosity. Philosopher noticed some books he had never seen before and began searching through them.

Dandy looked at the newspaper Black Crow had been reading. The headlines read **"The Gray Devils Again!" and "Rusty the Persian Headed to Town!"**

"Who are the Gray Devils and Rusty the Persian?" he asked.

Black Crow answered, "The Gray Devils are Wild McRat's Gang commanded by four brother rats. They keep all the rats banded so strong that nobody can do anything against them. The poor cats can do nothing to stop them; they're such a well-organized gang. Those four brothers know all the cat customs. Lots of kittens have gone missing; cats have even died and there's been fighting everywhere – all because of the ideas and actions of those rats."

"Where are they now?" asked Snow with a trembling voice.

"They live in a very big place named Don'tGive-ADamn Lodge. It's a well-guarded place outside of town. And the cats are staying in Consolation Camp, located on the top of the biggest tree.

"Catfish!" swore Wandering Sheriff. "Rusty the Persian is the meanest gunslinger this side of the Mississippi. As his name hints, he's a rust-colored Persian with the flattest face I've ever seen. Really mean-looking. I've had a showdown with him before. He'll use any trick to get his gun out faster. When

I met up with him, I barely escaped. But just in time I saw him move his paw down to his holster and I knew I wasn't going to make it, so I jumped to the side of the nearest building before he could say 'pickled mice,' and got out of town fast. Haven't heard a whisker of him since...until now."

"Can we do anything?" asked Rascal.

"We must go to Seven Cats Creek and bring to town all the cats that live there," said Black Crow. "They are miners, looking for gold. Then we have to go to Old Cat Crossing and Wild Cat Creek. Then to Hairball Summit, where there are cats farming catnip and raising mice. We have to warn them about the rats. Wild McRat's Gang is attacking every single cat. They want to destroy all cats. As for Rusty, I had the faint hope that he might be here to help us with the rats, but I honestly don't think that's going to happen. I'm suspicious about his reason to be here. We must be alert. Keep an eye out for him."

"I'll take Dandy, Snow and Sofia with me and go to End of Trail, Dead Mouse Point and to Smoke in the Valley," he added.

"Rascal, Philosopher, Bunny and Lumby will go with me to the rest of the places," said Wandering Sheriff. "After we warn all the cats there, we also have to get up to Angry Cat Pass."

Suddenly a strange voice behind them said, "I'll go with Wandering's group."

All the cats turned toward the voice. What a surprise! It was the old cat, Uncle Toothless.

"What are you doing here, Uncle?" asked Rascal.

"Well, I saw you guys sneaking around, so I thought it best to keep not only one eye on you, but both eyes...then, well...you know the rest...I'm here and ready to help those cats. I have lots of experience fighting with the rats. I've lost a few of my teeth on them. My Wild West name is DeadYetAlive!"

"What do you think about Rusty the Persian being in town, Uncle?" asked Wandering Sheriff.

"Now there's a sneaky gunslinger if I ever saw one," Uncle replied. "We have to be especially keen on his movements."

3

The cats spent all that day running from place to place to warn everyone. They gathered together in a hideout named Treasure Trove close to Catfish Lake and very close to town.

At one point, they were wandering along the dusty streets when the Butterfield Stagecoach arrived. Three humans and one black dog with a red collar got down. Rascal watched intently and saw something that looked like a small piece of paper drop from the dog's collar. The dog did not notice. After it went off, Rascal picked up the piece of paper and almost let out a yowl while he read it. He ran straight to Wandering Sheriff and showed it to him. It said, "Pony Express arriving in town tomorrow. All rats should be ready for action. When nobody is around, neither human nor animal, rats should use their sharp teeth to cut through all the belts connected to the saddle. No more Pony Express!"

"I don't understand," said Rascal, scratching his ear.

Wandering Sheriff tried to explain. "The Pony Express is the greatest enterprise of modern times. I mean today, as in the year 1860!"

"Why?" asked Rascal, still confused.

"Let me explain it this way. The Butterfield Stagecoach travels 2000 miles in 21 days, but the Pony Express does the same 2000 miles in 10 days."

"How?"

"Each of the riders gallops full tilt for 35 to 75 miles, then passes the mail to the next relay rider, speeding throughout the day and night without stopping. The riders are local heroes. Crowds of humans cheer them off each time. They are adventurous young kids with nothing to lose and with dreams of adventure and glory spurring them on. Soon to be historical legends, William (Buffalo Bill) Cody and James Butler (Wild Bill) Hickok were both Pony Express Riders," said Wandering Sheriff. "Now the rats want to ruin everything because they don't like our civilization."

"Okay, so we have to be very watchful of those rats," said Rascal nodding, and he scampered off with the note.

4

After Rascal had gone, one lone cat slowly emerged from the stagecoach. He stood in the dusty road and looked around in all directions, his eyes squinting against the hot afternoon sun that shone off his rust-colored fur. Unconsciously, his paw lowered to rest on the holster of his six-shooter. *This looks like a peaceful town,* he thought. *I'm ready for some rest. I'm tired of looking over my shoulder all the time. This town looks like just the right place for me to retire my guns.*

And Rusty the Persian headed off to look for a decent hotel with a hot bath and a soft bed.

5

"Now, Rascal," said the sheriff, "go to Treasure Trove and tell all the cats to be ready for tomorrow's action against the rats. They have to come to the place where the Pony Express will arrive and watch out for them all. For the rest of today I'll teach you guys how to shoot pistols and use a lasso."

It was lots of fun for Rascal and the rest. Each of them took a Wild West name. Snow was Calamity Jane, Dandy was Gentleman Joe, Bunny was Catbear, Lumby – Canmore, and Sofia – Bumble Bee. But Sofia did not want to shoot with pistols or guns; she was afraid of the noise they made so she chose a bow and arrows. Rascal and Philosopher did not have Wild West names yet, but they promised to think about some.

That night, Rascal announced that his new name was Wind Rider and Philosopher said, "I'm Sitting Cat."

Wandering Sheriff had found a bunch of cowboy hats locked away in a closet in a room behind the sheriff's office. There was enough of them for all the cats. Rascal looked quite dapper in his black hat with a white band and feather. Philosopher couldn't quite keep his hat on because every time he thought deeply about somethings, which he often did, his ears moved from front to back and from back to front, which kept the hat from sitting properly on his head. Lumby's hat fell over his face and covered his eyes. He had to push it back up on his head. The others had hats that fitted just fine. They all looked quite menacing, even though they did not feel that way, but they hoped the rats would surely be intimidated by the 'cowcats'.

Just then, one cat rushed into the office. "Where's...Wandering Sheriff?" he panted, holding onto the edge of Black Crow's desk.

"I'm back here, Jax. What is it? You look as if you've seen a ghost!"

"Rusty the Persian's...in town. I saw him...go into...the Hearthrug Hotel," Jax said between breaths. "I got here...as fast as I could. What do we do, Sheriff?"

"I guess there's nothing left but for me to go and pay him a visit," Wandering Sheriff said.

"You can't go alone," said Black Crow. "I'll go with you."

After some thought, Wandering Sheriff said, "Well, okay, but I think it best if you wait outside. I don't want him thinkin' I'm lookin' for trouble. Besides, I'll need you to keep a lookout in case he tries to make a run for it."

When they arrived at the Hearthrug Hotel, Wandering Sheriff lingered awhile out front, preparing himself for whatever might come. *What reason could Rusty the Persian possibly have for coming into town? Does he know that I'm here and has come to finish the job he failed to do so long ago? How could that be? How could he know?*

After a few minutes, noticing Black Crow getting a bit edgy, he pushed open the doors into the bar and looked around. There were a few patrons at the bar, a few tables occupied, but not a full house. He swaggered over to the barkeep and asked, in a quiet meow, which room Rusty the Persian was staying in. The barkeep stifled a gasp, slowly looked around to make sure no one else could hear, and raised his eyes up toward the balcony to the door of Room #5.

Wandering Sheriff swished his whiskers in thanks and padded up the stairs. Taking a deep breath, and waving his tail once, he quietly knocked on the door.

"Who is it?" came a gruff meow.

"I'm the sheriff of this town here, Rusty, and I want to have a few words with you if you don't mind."

"Well, as a matter of fact, I do mind, sheriff. I'm not botherin' anyone. Just mindin' my own business. Now leave me be."

"Can't do that, Rusty. Just wanna' have a few friendly words with you. Now let me in, or I'm gonna' have to shoot off the doorknob."

For a few minutes, there was no sound coming from inside the room. Wandering Sheriff was beginning to think that Rusty had sneaked out through the window. But he knew Black Crow was outside in case such an idea occurred to him.

Finally, just as he was raising his gun to shoot off the knob, he heard the key in the lock turn and the door creaked slowly open. He was face to face with Rusty the Persian. Rusty looked older than the last time he had seen him, older and tired, real tired.

"Well, Sheriff, what can I do for you?" Rusty asked.

"You're lookin' pretty tired, Rusty. "What brings you to our lovely town?"

"Look, Sheriff, like I said, I'm just mindin' my own business. I'm just here for a little relaxation."

"Really? I can't help but think that's not your only reason for being here. After all, with your track record, can you blame me?"

Rusty eyed Wandering Sheriff for a moment, sizing him up before answering, trying to decide how much to tell him. He looked like a decent cat. After all, he had the courage to come right up to his door and stay until he let him in. "I'm gonna be honest with you, Sheriff. All I ask is you keep this between me and you."

"You have my word, Rusty."

"It's been a long time since I could trust anyone's word." Rusty scratched his tattered ear, waved his tail a time or two and said, "I've decided to retire, Sheriff. Yup, I'm retiring my guns."

This was the last thing that Wandering Sheriff

expected to hear from Rusty the Persian, the meanest, cruelest gunslinger in these parts for as long as he could remember. He had to stop a minute and let his mind work out what he was hearing. Rusty the Persian retiring his guns! Then it hit him. Maybe he could talk Rusty into joining them against the enemy, the rats. Just one last gunfight. Rusty could go out doing some good for a change. Maybe his faint hope could be a reality!

6

The next day the rats were very surprised to see a lot of cats milling about. Much to their surprise, the Pony Express started its journey without any problems. The rats were angry. They did not know how the cats had done it, but they knew it was, indeed, they who had foiled their plan. They wanted revenge...soon.

"Now you see, Wind Rider," said Wandering Sheriff to Rascal, calling him by his Wild West name, "you have to write about that because humans don't know what we did to prevent awful disasters from happening."

That evening, as Rascal was taking a walk along the main road in town, two rats ambushed him. He yowled loud enough for the rest of the cats to hear him. Before long there was a huge brawl, cats against rats, in the middle of the dusty road. The horses, who found the rats very distasteful, shook their loosely tied reins from the poles and galloped into the street, intent upon stomping on any rats they could.

The cats were pleasantly surprised to have new-found allies. They were beginning to be overwhelmed by the swarm of rats and were grateful for the horses' help. As the horses joined the brawl, the rats were concentrating so much on avoiding being squashed by their hooves that they could not fight the cats. It wasn't long before they were outnumbered and when they realized they could not win, they retreated to their hideout.

"Thank you, Pardners," said Wandering Sheriff. "Those rats were just starting to get the best of us when you showed up. Sure do appreciate the help. You know, I just happen to have some sugar cubes in the sheriff's office. I found 'em when I was looking for these here cowboy hats. They might be a little old, but they're sugar."

"You're very welcome, Wandering Sheriff. We can't stand those rats. They try to take over every-thing," said the obvious leader of the horses, whose name was Polo. Behind him, the other horses whin-nied and snorted in agreement.

As Wandering Sheriff and the other cats fed the sugar cubes to their new friends, they found out that the actions of the rats were affecting not only the cats in town, but the other animals and the humans as well. The cows were constantly finding them in their feed. They, too, would gladly have helped stomp on the rats, given the chance. The farmers left traps around the barns where the cattle feed was stored and sometimes they caught a few. The 50 cats felt stron-ger against about 250 rats, now that they had allies.

Meanwhile, Rusty had watched the brawl from his second floor window, still pondering Wandering Sheriff's request. The cats seemed to do alright against the rats, although without the horses' help, it may not have turned out so well for them. Maybe he *could* help them. Maybe he'd be remembered for this one good thing he would do instead of all the bad things he'd been doing. *Maybe...just maybe,* he thought.

7

The next day the rats came up with what they thought was a solution to the disputes between rats and cats. They arrived at the sheriff's office and told the cats that they wanted peace and for that reason they invited all of them to their place to dance.

Uncle Toothless announced that he was tired and needed a cat nap, so he would not be going to the ball with the rats. "Besides," he murmured, so only the cats could hear, "I don't believe one word those sneaky rats say. We must be very wary. They have something else in mind, mark my words."

A small rat named Slide Out told Rascal and his group that he would show them where there were mice that were very easy to catch. Stand Off, a bigger rat, nodded his head in agreement. "I know about those mice. They aren't quite all dead yet and they really are very easy to catch."

"A curious and engaging animal, the sidehill mouse," said Slide Out. "Sidehill mice were once plentiful in the hills, though I fear they are now nearing extinction, especially in this area."

"What do they look like?" asked Rascal, curiously, forgetting the old saying that curiosity killed the cat.

Stand Off said, "The right-hand variety, you mean?"

Slide Out added, "There is also the left-hand variety."

"Which ones are easier to catch?" asked Snow and Dandy.

Restless, Rascal walked around with both his curiosity and now excitement.

"It means both of their right legs are longer than the left. They can only walk the hills in a counter-clockwise direction. However, there are an even larger number of left-handed sidehill mice. They only walk in a clockwise direction. Then behind the Rat's Pass lives the high-behinded sidehill mouse. It travels only uphill."

"Wow!" shouted Lumby.

"I don't believe it," said Philosopher suspiciously

"I know, town cats like you – City Slickers – don't know about them," said Stand Off. And Slide Out added, "Don't forget to mention about the low-be-hinded sidehill mouse. They only walk downhill."

Uncle Toothless said, "Don't trust rats! They are rats! I won't go, even though those mice might be tasty and pink, like ice cream. Besides, my legs ache. I've done lots of walking instead of lots of sleeping like I usually did in my old house." Uncle turned around and to himself he said, "...mice that taste like chocolate or vanilla or...high-behinded mice...ha, ha, ha...they must think we're stupid."

"Where are Sheriff and the others?" asked Sofia.

"They've gone hunting for those side-hill mice," said a big rat with a friendly smile and a smaller rat added, "Let's go before it gets too late."

Uncle Toothless tried once more to prevent Rascal and the others from following the rats. "Don't be so quick to follow them. Like I said, they're up to something."

"But they're going to lead us to mice," said Rascal. "Tasty mice. Mmmmm. What harm can there be?"

"Watch out," called Uncle in a final warning.

8

Rascal was very excited and quickly forgot about his dream of the night before. He had dreamed about huge danger and as he discovered, the danger of death in the Wild West was ever present and took many forms. But in his dream the danger had only one form – RATS! He dreamed that all the cats, humans, cows and horses were changed into rats. It bothered him for about two seconds but then he easily dismissed it and happily followed the two rats, letting the idea of catching a mouse or two cloud his better judgment. *Besides, if Wandering Sheriff has already left to hunt the mice,* he thought, *it will be safe for them, too. Maybe Uncle was being a bit too cautious.*

Philosopher thought about staying behind with Uncle Toothless because he, too, was not convinced that the rats were sincere. But he thought he would be better able to help the others if something did happen, so he followed along.

They went behind Cat Valley towards Angry Cat Pass. There were some mice on the meadow but the rats said they were not the ones they were looking for.

That did not matter to the cats. They got into pounce position, but the rats interrupted their concentration.

"These are not the mice we're after," they said. "Let's go find the real juicy mice."

Reluctantly, the cats continued to follow the rats. After an hour or so, they saw coyote tracks, lynx tracks, rabbit tracks and squirrel tracks, but no mice tracks.

Suddenly the rats shouted, "Run! Faster! Let's go!"

The cats followed their leader when suddenly they were airborne. First Rascal, then the rest of the cats. With a jolt of surprise they found that they had fallen into an old mine hole. The rest of the cats were there with Wandering Sheriff. He looked up in puzzlement. Around the rim of the hole lots of rats were leering down at them with evil grins.

"Anything that can go wrong will go wrong," said Wandering Sheriff.

"And here we are, feeling as if we'd all been hit on the head," Rascal added.

Philosopher sat, thinking his deep thoughts; thoughts not known to others.

"Dudes! Dudes! Ha, ha! There are also mice that have colors like pheasant but taste like duck or even small deer," jeered the rats.

And this is only the beginning, Sofia thought miserably. She did not know whether to be sorry or fearful or angry or if she should just cry. Poor lady-cat, she got hysterical in the way that well-bred cats will do.

Rascal asked Sheriff, "You were looking for those side-hill mice too?"

Wandering Sheriff opened his eyes wide. "What? Side-hill mice? What is this nonsense? I was chasing those bad guys. They told me they found a big trap where some cats had fallen down and I ran here to rescue them."

Rascal remembered what Uncle Toothless had said and felt foolish for believing the rats.

"Why are there no kittens, except for that orange one that looks like a miniature Wandering Sheriff?" asked Snow.

"That one is my son," said Sheriff, proudly.

"I want to rescue our brothers and sisters and friends," said Yellow Nugget, the oldest son of Wandering Sheriff and White Mist, a white cat who was standing silently not too far away.

"They are being held as prisoners somewhere in this mine. And it's very sad because the rats are raising them like rats. Then they use them to carry out their evil plans. The poor kittens think they are rats. Only I escaped from them and I know I'm very proud to be a cat!" Meanwhile the rats became bored of harassing the cats and left. Not too long after, the cats heard the voice of Uncle Toothless. "I knew those rats were up to no good."

"I knew you'd come, Uncle Toothless! I'm sorry we didn't listen to your warning," called Rascal.

"I was often in trouble too, a long time ago when I was young. And I learned one thing: there's always a solution to everything… But…for now…I have an idea. Each one of you, push a stone to one side of the wall. Then keep doing that until they are piled up high enough so you can climb out."

The cats did that while Yellow Nugget went off to search for his brothers and sisters.

9

Meanwhile an old rattlesnake smelled something new outside of his rock. He was not sure if he wanted to venture outside of his warm little hole, since it was already dusk, but the smell was very interesting and he had not been able to catch anything for a while. He was hungry. Slowly he slithered out just enough to let his forked tongue feel the breeze, since that was where his sense of smell was, in his tongue. He got a stronger scent and headed in that direction.

Soon he came across an old creature gesturing near an open mine pit where he had often found food still half-alive at the bottom. After the prey fell in, it usually hurt itslef enough not to be able to move very far. That only made his job easier, as he had lost one of his fangs in a horrific battle with a tarantula a year ago. He had a secret little hole that he used to wind his way to the bottom of the pit and sneak up on his unsuspecting prey. He knew there must be something down in the pit now. It would be easy to overtake whatever was at the bottom rather than try to attack this animal at the top, who seemed quite lively.

Surely whatever was at the bottom would be injured and would not be able to fight back, as this creature in front of him was quite able to do.

10

After all the stones were piled, the cats realized that there were not enough stones to reach the top. Sofia was on the verge of becoming hysterical again. Fortunately, Uncle Toothless noticed a small dead tree lying nearby and dragged it to the top of the hole. He carefully slid it down so it wedged into some rocks at the top of the pile. Now there was a complete path to the opening of the hole. Uncle felt useful and happy. He said, "Hit your problems from every angle. Try anything if it makes sense."

When the rattlesnake cautiously poked his head out from behind the small rock that covered his secret pathway, he was delighted at his good fortune for there, right in front of him, was a kitten. It was larger than his normal prey, but not too large that he could not swallow it. That would keep him satisfied for a very long time. He hissed.

Wandering Sheriff heard it, turned and quickly jumped in between the rattlesnake and Yellow Nugget. Face to face with the rattlesnake, he asked the others to carefully start climbing up the rocks to the top. Carefully, but quickly.

Yellow Nugget and White Mist insisted on staying behind and searching for the rest of the kittens.

Before Wandering Sheriff could protest, the rattlesnake struck. Wandering Sheriff instinctively jumped out of his way, but the rattlesnake caught Yellow Nugget in the leg and began to drag him toward his hole. Yellow Nugget yowled in pain. White Mist lunged at the rattlesnake and sliced his back with her claws. At that the rattlesnake let go of his hold on Yellow Nugget and raced back to his hole, never to be seen again.

Was it too late for Yellow Nugget? The venom had already begun to spread. His leg swelled up quickly.

"Uncle!" shouted Wandering Sheriff. "I need help. Do you know what to do about a rattlesnake bite?"

Uncle, in alarm, answered, "What's happened? What rattlesnake?"

"There was a rattlesnake hiding down here. He got Yellow Nugget, my son. We need to get the venom out of him quickly. There's not much time."

As Rascal made his way back down the pile of stones to help Wandering Sheriff lift Yellow Nugget up the stones and to the outside, Rusty the Persian sauntered up behind Uncle. No one noticed him until they brought Yellow Nugget out of the hole. As soon as Wandering Sheriff's head crested the rim, he caught sight of Rusty. They locked eyes for just a moment and in that moment, an unspoken agreement happened. Rusty would help them fight the rats. They nodded ever so slightly and swished their tails.

"I saw your cats following the rats out of town and knew there'd be trouble. So I followed," Rusty said to Wandering Sheriff.

"Appreciate that, Rusty. Much obliged."

Uncle looked confused. *Why is Wandering Sheriff talking to a known gunslinger? Why is he here?* But Uncle knew better than to question Wandering Sheriff's motives, so he kept his mouth shut.

Once they had Yellow Nugget lying on level ground, Uncle looked him over. "I'm not sure I can help you, Wandering Sheriff. This leg is mighty swollen."

Just then, Lumby began to purr softly. Bunny looked over at him in surprise. *Surely purring is not going to help now,* he thought. But even so, he joined Lumby in a low purring. Soon all the cats were purring, more because they did not know what else to do than because they thought it would help.

Rusty had never seen anything like what he was seeing. A group of cats all purring in unison! *What did they think they were doing?*

But soon some ants came to the surface drawn by the purring. Ants are immune to snake venom. They crawled up onto Yellow Nugget's leg and began to withdraw the venom. Slowly his leg shrunk, but it was still very red and sore. He could not walk on it. When the ants had finished and retreated to their holes, Wandering Sheriff said, "I never realized how powerful purring can be."

"Nor I," said Rusty, with much surprise.

When White Mist realized that her son was out of danger, she climbed back down into the hole to continue her search for the lost kittens. Her other children were among them and she needed to find them.

11

Meanwhile in town, the rats had bypassed the traps that had been laid for them and gotten into the storage barn, where all the grain and feed were stored. Some of them had fleas that carried a virus. The virus spread as the fleas jumped from one rat to another and as the rats fed, they spread the virus to the grain and feed. The virus was deadly to humans, so when the humans ate the grain, they became deathly ill. Doctors back then didn't have either the medical know-how that they have today, or the technology. So even with the best doctor, a human could die in a matter of days, maybe even hours in severe cases.

The humans that belonged to Polo, leader of the horses, were some of those who contracted this deadly disease. Polo was deeply concerned and called a meeting of all the animals – horses, cows and cats.

"Friends, my humans are very ill with a new sickness that we haven't seen before. I heard them talking. They think it's from the rats but they don't know how it's spreading to them."

"We should have run those rats out of town when

we had the chance," one of the other horses muttered.

"I agree," said Polo. "We must do that now. Otherwise, no one will be left in this town. What do you say cat friends? Do you have any ideas about how to do this?"

Philosopher had been thinking. His ears moved back and forth, first the right ear, then the left. How could they rid the town of the rats and save the humans from this deadly illness?

"Rascal," whispered Philosopher, "listen. I think the food in the barn might be the source of this horrible sickness. First, we must investigate."

Rascal looked at Philosopher with admiration. "I knew you'd have an idea about this." Then to Polo he said, "My brother, Philosopher, thinks that the food in the barn may be contaminated by the rats. We must first investigate that before we take any action. The cats will scout out the barn. If we find any rats in there, we'll question them. If all of you horses and cows could stand guard outside, just in case there are too many of them, that would be helpful."

Polo nodded in agreement with the plan, as the other horses and cows whinnied, snorted or mooed with approval.

"My friends, that's a wonderful idea. How did you know about this?" Polo asked.

"My brother is a very deep thinker and a reader of many books. He came upon the information in one of those books," said Rascal. "He learned that rats spread disease through food."

"Our Philosopher is very smart," said Sofia affectionately.

"Philosopher! Philosopher!" sang Lumby, happily.

"Tonight we'll watch the barn. That will be when they come out to eat, I think," said Rascal. "We'll meet there when the sun goes down."

12

That night, Wandering Sheriff, Rusty the Persian, Rascal, Philosopher and all the other cats crept toward the huge barn that housed the food for the town. Lumby stayed with Uncle Toothless because he was too young for such a stakeout and also just in case there were anymore rattlesnakes lurking about with a hankering for a kitten. As they approached the barn they heard squeaking and rustling. Wandering Sheriff raised his tail as a sign to stop and be very still. The squeaking and rustling continued, so Sheriff signaled for Rascal, Philosopher, Bunny, Sofia, Snow and Dandy to go around to the right side of the barn. He, Rusty and the rest of the cats went around the opposite side. The plan was to enter the barn from either end and take the rats by surprise. The horses and cows waited silently in the shadows around the barn.

But now they knew that Philosopher had been right: the rats were spreading the deadly virus through the food.

The cats slipped into the barn unnoticed by the rats. There was only a handful of rats crawling over the grain, instead of the swarm that they were afraid they would encounter. On Wandering Sheriff's signal, they pounced on the rats, cornering them.

"What are you doing in the humans' food?" asked Wandering Sheriff.

"We're doing you no harm," answered one of them. "We always come here to feed. Let us go or the rest of Wild McRat's gang will take revenge."

Polo, alerted by one cat that the rats had been successfully detained, stuck his head in the barn door and said, "But you <u>are</u> doing us harm. You are spreading a disease that's killing our humans. You must stop feeding here or we'll have to run you out of town."

Evil grins spread across the rats' faces. "You can't make us leave. We'll eat here as long as we like," said one of them. Then they recognized the face of Rusty the Persian, cruelest gunslinger in all history, and their evil grins melted into gaping mouths, their eyes full of fear.

Polo snorted in anger.

Just then, Philosopher said, "The only thing we can do now is destroy this grain. If it continues to be eaten, more humans will get sick."

"How can we destroy all this grain?" asked Wandering Sheriff.

"I think the only way is by fire," answered Philosopher.

"Fire!" gasped Polo. "That's a bit extreme, isn't it? How would we ever get a fire started? And then how would we ever stop it?"

"The only way to kill the virus is by fire. We can use a lantern from your humans' house to start the fire, Polo. Then I don't think we need to worry about putting it out. Humans are much more able to do that than we are," said Philosopher.

Rascal looked at Philosopher as he spoke. He wanted to remember all of this for his book. *Cats really did prevent disasters in the Wild West,* he thought. What an adventure!

Polo nodded hesitantly and went back to the other horses to relay the plan. With a whinny, one of them left the group and came back shortly with a lit lantern.

When the captured rats realized that the cats were serious, they tried to slip out of the barn while the cats were discussing what to do, and run to tell the rest of the gang what was happening; but mostly they wanted to alert the others that Rusty the Persian was in town…and helping the cats. But they weren't fast enough to outsmart Rusty. He knew they'd try to make a run for it and he had his six-shooter at the ready. Before the rats knew it, they were face to face with the barrel of his gun.

"Where do you vermin think you're going?" he asked, his grin wide.

The rats were petrified. The smallest one said, "Please, let us go. I'll tell you anything you want to know."

"Shut up, Rufus! said the largest rat. "Wild McRat

will have your head when he finds out!"

"I don't care! I don't want to be tortured! That's what you do to rats when you catch them, right?" Rufus asked Rusty.

Rusty only grinned wider.

Wandering Sheriff stepped in then. "Good job, Rusty. They would've escaped for sure and got word back to Wild McRat. We'll take them back to the jail. Jax will keep an eye on them."

Sofia caught Rusty's eye, smiled and swished her whiskers in thanks. Rusty was caught off guard. He never expected such a pretty cat to smile at him. He was used to seeing cats with scars and eyes missing and tails half cut off, all of them wanting to kill him, not smile at him. He could only nod.

"Sheriff," said Sofia, "if these rats don't return to their camp, they might send out others looking for them."

"They might, but it'll be too late," said Wandering Sheriff. "They won't harm any more humans with this disease. But we'll keep a lookout for them."

Sofia looked at least a little relieved and glanced up again at Rusty. This time he was ready and gave her what he thought was his best smile.

Wandering Sheriff waved his tail.

With that, Polo dropped the lantern into the barn. Immediately, flames rose from the grain. The cats, herding the rats, ran to the holes they came in through and slipped out into the night. Horses, cows, cats and rats all hid in the shadows nearby to watch the inferno.

Before long they heard shouts from the town. The humans had been alerted and were coming to see what the commotion was. Soon they would bring water, but Wandering Sheriff hoped it would not be before most of the grain had been destroyed. The cats slipped off into the night to deposit their prisoners.

13

The next day Polo called another meeting.

"Friends, our work last night was successful. All the contaminated grain was destroyed. However, one of my humans, a child, died during the night from the sickness. They'll bury him quickly, since the disease is so powerful. They don't want it to spread. How will we know that the sickness did actually come from the grain?" Polo looked at Philosopher as he asked this.

"In time, the humans who have the sickness will either die or get better. Hopefully, they'll all get better. But no more humans will get sick. We just have to make sure the rats leave town. I'm not exactly sure about the best way to make them leave, though," Philosopher answered.

"Just leave that to me, Pardner," said Wandering Sheriff, with a wink in Rusty's direction. "A battle is what's called for here. A regular, no holds barred, knockdown battle. That's what'll make those rats leave town. We'll muster up all the cats in town. Horses and cows, too, if they want to join in." He paused, twirled his whiskers in his paws, waved his tail a few times and continued. "At this point, I'm going to take this opportunity to introduce a new friend who's here to help us in our battle against the rats. Many of you may know him as Rusty the Persian."

A unified gasp went up in the crowd.

"I understand some of you may have doubts about Rusty's loyalty. But let me assure you, he's on our side."

There were some discontented murmurs throughout the crowd. Sofia looked worried that Rusty would not be accepted. Snow and Dandy waved their tails in agitation that there were still some who did not trust Wandering Sheriff's judgement.

Black Crow stepped up next to Wandering Sheriff. "Cats! Listen! Hear me out!"

The crowd quieted down and gave their attention to Black Crow.

"I was there last night at the barn when we captured the rats who were poisoning the humans' food. They would've escaped if it hadn't been for Rusty. He was quick enough to suspect that they'd make a run for it. We can use his keen abilities to get the better of those dastardly rats. Please, give him a chance."

The crowd was quiet for a few moments, then a dull murmur filled the room. One cat, a large one, called out, "I'll give him a chance!" Then one after another they called out the same, "I'll give him a chance," until they surrounded Rusty, patting him on his shoulder, twining their tails with his, accepting him into the group.

Sofia was glad. Rusty looked over in her direction and gave her the biggest, brightest cat smile he had ever given anyone. In fact, he could not even remember when he had ever smiled. It felt good.

Lumby asked, "Can I be in the battle too? I'm not too small for that, am I?"

"A battle is not something you'd want to be in, Lumby. There must be another way," said Bunny.

"Purring is another way," Lumby said.

Bunny looked at Lumby with a smile. "Purring is a good way, Lumby. I hope Wandering Sheriff and Rusty agree."

Meanwhile, the townspeople were beginning to clear away the debris from the burned barn and build a new one. The town's doctor suspected that the grain had been somehow involved in the disease, but was not sure exactly how. At his suggestion, this time the barn was built tight, with no holes for rats to get in, or any other creature, for that matter.

14

The next day, the cats went looking for the rats. Rascal told Wandering Sheriff about his dream and Sheriff answered, "You may have had a dream about a battle in the past, or one that may yet happen, or one that will never happen. But if that was about a battle that may yet happen, you'd better be prepared for those rats."

Vultures began to fill the sky. They already began to smell the blood of war. They knew that soon there would be dead from both sides, plentiful enough to feed all of them.

Bunny looked with fear at the vultures and said to Sheriff, "I know the best way to win every battle without using arms or spilling blood. By purring. And, as you already know, Lumby is our champion purrer."

Sheriff studied Bunny as a botanist might study a new plant. A gray cat named Old Dust approached with a smaller one named Young Dust. Old Dust looked at Sheriff and asked, "What's wrong? You look as if you've seen your father's ghost."

Black Crow stood loyally by his sheriff and answered, "Wandering Sheriff is a good cat in many ways, but new things disconcert him. His eyes turn yellow when he's held by some strong emotion. In fact, they are yellow now..."

A black and white cat approached. "Sheriff, we'll come with you and if we have to die, we'll still come with you."

Rascal looked around and said, "Yeah, you promised that we could die together. But I don't want to die. Purring is the best way to win this battle."

"I don't think purring is going to stop 250 angry rats. Let's go fight! Follow me!" Sheriff shouted angrily.

Rusty took a moment to prepare for what he knew would be his last gunfight ever in this life. He glanced over at Sofia, wondering how she was feeling, but she was in the middle of a group of cats and did not see him. He looked down at his belt, a holster filled with a six-shooter on either side, and smiled grimly. He did not know how many rats there were, but he knew there was a chance the cats might not win this one. He had never been in a fight he did not win. *Funny what life throws at you, where you end up,* he thought. *Me, a gunfighter most of my life, and here I am almost dreading what might prove to be my most famous gunfight ever.* He checked his guns and headed over to where Sofia's group was.

Bunny tried to smile, but he was not sure how successful he was. Lumby, Sofia, Dandy, Snow,

Philosopher and Rascal, along with Bunny, seemed to move very slowly, or perhaps their feet moved at a reasonable pace, but their minds could not keep up.

Sofia looked up to see Rusty nearby and maneuvered herself next to him.

"How are you holding up?" he asked her.

"Better than I thought," she said. "But I still feel butterflies in my stomach. I'm scared. Those rats are such nasty creatures."

"That they are," Rusty agreed. "But we have some of the best cat fighters. And the horses and cows, too. We'll do fine." He hoped he sounded more convincing than he felt.

Rascal muttered something that was better not said aloud, so he whispered in Philosopher's ear, "Let's purr, brother."

Sofia was looking ahead and thought dark thoughts but before she started purring she said, "From now on I'm not Bumble Bee, but Bloody Sofia and I will kill those rats." Her voice was muffled because of her fear and anger.

Two hundred rats were waiting, ready to fight and 50 cats were walking in their direction to certain death.

The City Slickers, Dandy, Snow, and the others started to purr and with every second they purred louder and stronger. But it did not seem to matter. The battle was imminent. The rats were not slowing down. They swarmed around the 50 cats, armed with knives and swords, their sharp teeth showing through evil grins.

"At least we tried," said Sofia. Her voice sounded low and hollow and her head felt woolly. Rusty gave her one last smile before heading off to the center of the swarm of rats, his six-shooters blazing, rats falling to his left and right.

Bunny had one arm around Lumby, holding off three rats, all the while continuing to purr.

Philosopher and Rascal had taken on a pack of 10 rats. Rascal was slightly cut by one of the rats' swords. His purring did not deter the rats.

Uncle Toothless and Wandering Sheriff were in the midst of the rats, back to back, slicing through the pack, a sword in one paw and a pistol in the other.

Suddenly a strange rumbling sound came from afar. Both rats and cats stopped fighting and looked up to see a cloud of dust quickly approaching.

"Stampede!" shouted Wandering Sheriff.

"Stampede!" shouted a rat.

It was certainly a stampede, but with only three cows – Matylda, Clara and Mua. They heard the purr of the cats and ran to them because they loved that sound so much.

The rats did not want to be squashed by hundreds of cows running wildly and trampling everything in their path. But with all the dust they could not see that there were only three cows. They all ran to the river and jumped in, squeaking with fear and panic. The current in the river was strong and carried them far away. They were not seen again, either by human or animal.

15

"That's what few City Slickers in Wild West Country would have done," said Rascal. He had finished his new book and called it "Wildly Wild West."

Philosopher took a look at the book. "Where did you find a photo of Sheriff?"

Rascal smiled. "It's me. Wandering Sheriff had no photo of himself. He may have been camera shy. Since he looks almost like me, I put my photo on the first page. I covered the black speckles on my nose with white flour so it would look okay!"

"Rascal. One more thing. Who gave you that sheriff star, the one you carry round your neck?"

"Oh, brother! A dead cat gave it to me. But of course he wasn't dead when he gave it to me," said Rascal. "Let's go see our Wandering Sheriff and show him the book."

The cats went to the place where they met the Ghost Cat for the first time. But nobody was there, so they went farther into the town. This time it was only a ghost town. Rascal would have liked to show his writing to Wandering Sheriff but there was nothing there, only a few walls of the empty sheriff's office and ruined houses. Catfish Lake was still there, the mountains were still there with more trees. There were no horses or cows. Or rats.

Up in the sky they saw a rainbow. Walking on the rainbow to the other side was Wandering Sheriff. He stopped, looked down and smiled at the cats. Then he finished walking slowly to the end.

Rascal knew that Wandering Sheriff was now in peace and happy on the other side of the rainbow and that he, Rascal, had done a great job! He hoped that Wandering Sheriff would see Grandma Calico and tell her how much they all thought about her. On the way back he found an old book and opened it. Its title was

"Self-Help Study for Kittens who Think They are Rats."

The book was very old, but Rascal took it home with him to read and to rewrite it. It was written by Yellow Nugget, son of Wandering Sheriff, with help from White Mist.

Part 2

Tale of The Oregon Trail

16

The next day the cats went to look around the ghost town some more. After walking around in the hot sun all day searching for treasures they got tired and slept in an old wagon before going back home.

As they lay sleeping in the quiet of the night, the terrible cry of a woman woke them up. A big brown horse had broken loose from an old man who was trying to harness him. The horse charged wildly and people scattered in all directions. The huge animal was rushing straight toward a small girl who was sleeping peacefully on the ground, directly in its path and blissfully unaware of the impending danger. Horrified, a few people dashed off toward the girl but the horse was too close – they were not going to reach her in time!

Suddenly, an orange ball of fur sprang from the wagon toward the path of the galloping horse and the sleeping girl. Rascal to the rescue! The brave cat was making a wild attempt to stop the out of control animal. The horse's hooves thundered toward heroic Rascal and seemed about to crush him...when, to everyone's surprise, it stopped in its tracks, looked Rascal straight in the eye and stepped carefully and slowly over him and the girl. Then it ran off.

A group of men chased after it, shouting for it to stop. The girl's mother ran toward her child to make sure she was okay. She shouted out thanks to God and crying happy tears she bent down to pat Rascal on the head. He purred serenely. "Thank you, brave cat," the grateful woman said.

Rascal looked at the girl. She was the same age as his beloved owner, Diana, about 11 years old, but this girl was fragile and her face was pale. The blond hair gave her face an even paler look. She opened her eyes, looked at Rascal, smiled and reached out her hand to touch his orange fur. Her mother was overjoyed. She knew that it was a miracle and in her heart she was sure the girl was going to be okay.

"Whose cat is this?" came a harsh voice from a group of three approaching horsemen.

"We don't know," answered some of the people who had gathered about. They all said they had never seen him before.

"It must be chased off. We can't take it with us on the Oregon Trail."

"That's the law!" added a small fat guy with a round, clean shaved head. "No cats allowed!"

"Please, I'll take care of him," pleaded the small girl.

Rascal watched everything very carefully as the humans continued their animated discussion. "What's your name?" a tall and very thin man asked the girl.

"Cynthia. And this is my older brother Lou," she said, pointing to the boy standing to her right. "Please, it's only one cat."

"That's enough! One cat leads to another. Soon we'll have more cats than horses on this trail. The place for a cat is on the farm catching mice, not traveling with pioneers."

More people surrounded the cat and the girl and they began a spirited discussion about the problem of having a cat on the wagon train trip. The rest of the cats were still hiding inside the covered wagon, waiting anxiously to hear what would happen next. The leader of the train group stepped forward and said, "Where did this cat come from?"

"It seems that he was hiding in my wagon," said the girl's father, a tall man with a big mustache, and he quickly added, "I'll take care of him. He saved my girl and I won't allow you to kick him away."

Just at that moment a mouse scurried out from under the wagon and hid under some nearby bushes.

"Look, mice!" someone shouted. "We can't afford to have them nibbling away at our food supply. Maybe we should take the cat. After all, nothing scares away mice like a cat."

"Oh, yeah, and maybe this super cat will also protect us from the bear, wolf and buffalo stampede…" somebody joked, and there was a roar of laughter from the crowd.

"Okay, you convinced me," said the leader in a good-natured voice. "You convinced me, but remember, when we run low on supplies we'll get rid of it."

"Or I'll eat it!" said somebody from behind. Everybody chuckled and then they returned to their jobs of preparing the wagons for the longest trip of their lives. And, they all hoped, the most exciting one.

17

While Rascal was purring in Cynthia's arms, the rest of his friends were still hidden under the hay among a few sacks of flour and bacon on the wagon. They were quietly carrying on an intense discussion about what to do next. Sofia wanted to go back to her room but did not know how. Philosopher was still trying to figure out what happened and why. Dandy and Snow were sleeping. Lumby, however, said only one thing: "I need to pee!" Hoping to remain undetected, Bunny helped him to go unnoticed under the wagon where there was enough sand, and then they rejoined the others. None of them could come to an agreement and they went right on talking, deep into the night.

While the humans were sleeping and the cats were bickering over their next step, all of a sudden a young yellow cat's face appeared at the back of the wagon. "Hi! Call me Wandering Kitty. I must check who you are since I'm checking everything in this train," said the kitten. "I'm going West!"

Rascal smiled. Philosopher jostled him and whispered in his ear, "He looks a lot like Wandering Sheriff from our previous adventure. He talks the same. I think we've come a little farther back in time and he's just a kitten." Then, speaking a bit more loudly, he asked their new friend, "What time is it? Oh, I mean, what year is it?"

"It's spring, 1848," answered the yellow kitty. "We are now in the jumping off town called Independence where the wilderness begins. We have to wait a few more days here."

Philosopher was intrigued. His ears perked up. "What for? Will more cats come?"

"Everybody is waiting for the grass to grow," said Wandering Kitty as if it were common knowledge.

The city slickers laughed, thinking this was a joke, but the country kitty explained: "If we went too early, the grass wouldn't be long enough for our oxen, horses and cows to graze along the way…"

"That's right! A mistake that could be fatal," added Rascal.

"What does 'jumping off' mean? Is it some kind of a dance?" asked Lumby, getting ready and hoping to perform it.

"It's the gathering point for wagon trains," said the kitty. "This is where the pioneers stock up their supplies and prepare their wagons. It's funny," he added with a smile, "the newcomers make friends and enemies here. They collect information about the trip, or misinformation, they don't know which one is the truth, and in general behave as though they were on a picnic."

"It's so crowded here," remarked Dandy, looking outside the wagon. "No wonder they want to leave this place."

"Yes and one of these humans spent four days just trying to find his friends!" said Wandering Kitty. "But soon we're going to the land where hot water shoots straight into the air and the earth bubbles as if it were boiling. No one believes me, not one cat and not even a dog. They thought I was telling tall tales and no cat that lives on our farm wanted to take this trip. They just chickened out and stayed with our new owner."

All the cats were looking at him with sympathetic eyes. They had been on too many adventures to be skeptical; they had seen and done so many things themselves that others would not believe. "I believe you, I know what hot springs mean," said Rascal, and the other cats nodded.

"How far is Ory-Gone and how will we get there? Why are we on a wagon tail?" asked Lumby, stumbling over his words as usual.

"Our Oregon Tail...I mean Oregon Trail, will wind its way west from Independence following the Big Blue and the Little Blue River to the Platte River. Then it will follow along the North Platte to the Sweetwater, then up and over the Continental Divide of the Rocky Mountains at South Pass, approximately the halfway marker of the journey. Then the trail follows the Snake River until it reaches the Columbia River, which flows into the Pacific. It's only 2000 miles," explained Wandering Kitty.

The cats were astonished at the yellow kitten's knowledge and how well he was prepared to go west. They felt they were now ready for the journey too – and it is always so exciting when a new adventure is just beginning!

18

The next day, Cynthia, with Lou and her mom Sara, discovered that they were richer in cats then they could have ever dreamed of. There were seven on their wagon! Her dad, Isaac, smiled and said, "Actually it's six and a half because of this small little black and white kitten." Lumby purred in his cute little way, as the man picked him up and stroked his soft fur.

They decided to keep them all. Yes, the surprised visitors were going to help them after all. They were kind-hearted people and very impressed with the orange cat that had stopped the horse. They had never known anything like it.

Later on Lumby asked Bunny, "Please, tell me, will I grow up one day? I want to be a big cat! I'm not little or half a cat, right, Bunny?"

Bunny looked at little Lumby and nodded with a smile. "I was little, too, once. Don't worry, you'll grow up faster than you think."

That seemed to make Lumby happy and he broke into a new dance, which he called his "One-Day-I-Will-Grow-Up-And-Be–Big-And-Strong" dance.

19

The wagon train was ready for departure in the early morning of the second day. The campground was bustling with activity, as the pioneers rushed about here and there taking care of all of the last minute details just before their departure. The cats tried to stay out of sight of all the other humans except for this one family. Wandering Kitty was with his owners. They did not yet know that they had a cat with them because they were too busy preparing for the longest trip of their lives.

They had not seen the sun all day and as evening came on the clouds grew heavier and heavier. Soon a light drizzle changed to a downpour. "We're having our first experience of a prairie schooner in the rain!" Wandering Kitty informed them. The cats climbed back into the wagon, curled up on the rolls of bedding and listened to the heavy patter of rain. It was a calming, pleasant sound that Rascal always enjoyed hearing, especially when he was someplace inside, warm and dry.

"What's a schooner?" he asked.

"A Prairie Schooner is a half-sized version of the Conestoga wagon. All four wheels have iron 'tires' to protect the wooden rims...and don't touch the canvas!"

Wandering Kitty warned Lumby who, they all knew, was keenly tempted to do precisely that.

"Why not?" asked the curious kitten, who, like most kittens, was never willing to let the word "don't" go unchallenged.

"If you touch it, the canvas will leak," Wandering Kitty explained.

"I'll try touching it as an experiment," Lumby said quietly, cocking his head to the side like a naughty child, then smiling and closing his eyes ready to sleep. When the other cats were not looking he touched the canvas and to his surprise his paw got wet. The water started dripping onto his nose and eyes. "I'll never do that again," he murmured to himself. (So many lessons just have to be learned the hard way).

20

The following day was busier even than the day before. The cats were wondering if there was any end to the boundless energy these folks seemed to have. Everybody was busy taking advantage of their final opportunity to shop and pick up some hints about traveling. The cats sat quietly in the corner of the wagon and listened to Wandering Kitty, who was explaining about his family selling the farm in order to travel to the 'Land of Promise.' "All winter they had talked about going out West. It seemed that Oregon must be the most wonderful spot in the world. They talked about the climate where the winters are warm. They talked about…about rich soil, and gold mines… I watched them making wagon covers, clothes for travel – all by hand."

"By hand? They make their clothes all by hand?" asked Sofia, fascinated by this ingenuity.

"Of course, they still don't have sewing machines," said Rascal, reminding her of how far back in the past they were now, in an era long before modern household appliances.

"What's wrong with not having sewing machines?" asked Philosopher. "Sewing by hand is a very old form of art, from over 20,000 years ago. The first thread was made of animal sinew, the first sewing needle was made of bones and animals' horns," he explained.

The others, as usual, marveled at their good friend's knowledge, though they did not necessarily exactly understand every word he was saying…but he sure was smart.

Wandering Kitty continued. "Finally, after sorting and packing food for six months, it was time to begin our journey and say goodbye to our friends and neighbors. Words of advice and warnings of all the dangers waiting for us on the trail still ring in my ears. I love my human family – father and mother and nine children, from two years old to 18. I love them all so I decided to go with them. I see you are traveling with Cynthia and Lou. They are very well tamed kids."

The cats were getting excited about what lay ahead of them and they were eager to leave as soon as possible. They watched with great interest as many of the people continued buying supplies for the trip and loaded their small wagons to the brim. It looked as if they might collapse under all the weight.

"It's just a simple small farm wagon!" Rascal exclaimed. "How can it possibly carry so much?"

"It's a technologically advanced vehicle," answered the kitten proudly. "This wagon can turn easily thanks to the complex undercarriage centered around a kingpin, which allows the front wheels to pivot. And look, the front wheels are smaller than the ones in back, which helps the wagon to round sharp corners. Most wagons have a toolbox on the side, a water barrel and hardwood brakes."

Philosopher was wide eyed as he gazed at the wagons. He was in awe of such fine engineering... who knew that such wonderful capabilities existed way back in the 1800s? These wagons were truly amazing travel vehicles, and he likened them to a 19th century version of modern day 747 jumbo jets.

The day went by without adventure but that didn't mean it was boring. The cats learned a lot about things that were new to them. It was like being in a living history museum.

After supper Wandering Kitty said, "Goodnight, and be ready for a lot of excitement tomorrow. Be sure to get plenty of sleep, because we have a long journey ahead of us."

The cats did not yet know what excitement there would be, except for starting the journey on 1 May 1848. They had a hard time getting to sleep that night, but eventually they all were away in Dreamland, conjuring up visions of the Oregon Trail. Except for Rascal. He still had work to do. Shortly after sunset, while the others lay sleeping quietly (except for Bunny's loud snoring!), he wrote in his diary:

Today I was hiding under the wagon. A few people were talking. The language of these people I could scarcely understand. When they say "heap of water, heap of man or Virginia is heap sick" they are speaking of quantity. Mr. Isaac asked another man a simple question when he passed close by our wagon. "How does your wife today?" The answer came, "O! Today! My wife is mighty better, yesterday she was powerful weak. Yesterday was mighty bad for her..." Dear diary, I must say goodnight to you now because tomorrow I have to wake up early and we will go West!!!! Rascal, the mighty rascally cat!

He hid his small notebook in a secret place and joined the others to have a good sleep.

21

In the morning, when day broke with the rising of the golden sun, the first words the cats heard were, "Arise! Arise!" Then the mules made a noise, such as the cats had never heard, which aroused the whole camp at once. People were up and about in an instant, almost as fast as a blink of an eye.

"Did they train those mules or what?" said sleepy Rascal, yawning. Lumby was rubbing his eyes.

"I prefer our alarm clocks," murmured Sofia, with only one eye open.

"Yeah, right, Aunt Sofia! You always hated it when the alarm clock in our home rang," said Lumby as he scratched his tummy. Sofia ignored his remark, stretched until her bones creaked and got ready for the new day.

After eating a hurried breakfast, they heard, "Catch up! Catch up!" Everyone wanted to get started at the same time, which created a huge traffic jam. It was like the Los Angeles freeways during rush hour.

Wandering Kitty pointed to the left. "Look! Our neighbors, the greenhorns from the city back east.

Looks like they've never yoked an oxen team or driven a mule team before. Now they'll have a hard time…they've already bumped into a tree and tipped their wagon and they've only just started out."

People ran to help them right the wagon. "Look! They couldn't even get the mules to go in the right direction," said Wandering Kitty, dumbfounded by the newcomers' lack of knowledge.

The cats wanted to help but they did not know what to do. All they could do was watch. Mr. Isaac's wagon moved slowly, pulled by a fine team of dappled gray horses which were going west, but the unlucky greenhorns' wagon was going full speed to the east.

"What terrible traffic!" wailed Sofia, accompanied by Snow.

"Where are you hurrying to?" asked Rascal.

Wandering Kitty replied, "We have five or six months to reach our destination. Easy! Take your time."

"Whoever hates traffic, they will always find it, even in the wildest place," concluded Philosopher. It made him wonder what it was like back in the Stone Age, before the wheel had even been invented. He thought there were probably traffic jams of people on foot trying to get inside of their caves. It reminded him of that old adage: *The more things change, the more they stay the same.*

"Some people try to make the trip with only a simple wheelbarrow. Look at those around from the right side," shouted Wandering Kitty, pointing at them.

Rascal was stunned. "They're ready to push a fully

loaded wheelbarrow for 2000 miles?" The cats looked with astonishment as three of them passed the traffic jam and pushed ahead into an open, uncluttered area.

"Humans are very creative," decided Philosopher.

Rascal shouted, "Look!" The cats all turned and saw what looked like a cross between a sailboat and a wagon. "What is that strange contraption?" he asked.

"It's called a wind wagon," Wandering Kitty informed them.

Two wind wagons whizzed past only a few feet in front of them. "Wow! What's the speed?" asked Rascal.

"I guess it's about 15 miles per hour!"

"That's snail speed," scoffed Bunny. "Proper speed is about 100 miles per hour."

"You must be joking, right?" said the country kitten. "Even the oldest and wisest of cats here know that's not possible."

The cats from Catanada realized there was no way to adequately explain the tremendous speeds they were familiar with from their own time in the 21st century, so they did not have any further discussions about speed. They knew that they should keep the conversation on the level of their friend's.

Mr. Isaac, meanwhile, was still stuck in the traffic jam. Before noon another strange vehicle passed by. It was a handcart but it was pulled not pushed. "Those people are smarter, it's easier to pull than to push," remarked Wandering Kitty.

"They'll not go far," predicted Sofia, "because

human endurance has its limits. Oxen and horses and mules are stronger."

"And cats," added Lumby.

They all looked at him as if he had said something foolish, but he retorted, "Have you ever seen how strong a lion is? And lions, after all, are members of the cat family."

Philosopher laughed and said, "The lad has a good point. There is a reason our majestic cousin is called King of the Jungle."

22

The next day the traffic was not that heavy and they got behind two wagons filled with dirt and with trees sticking out. "That's an odd sight! I never imagined trees would travel with us," said Wandering Kitty.

"I guess they're not ordinary trees, they are more like cherry, apple, pear and plum trees," observed Rascal.

"We'll see if those sticks get to the end of this trip safely," said Sofia.

"I'll mark it in my diary," said Rascal, then he turned to Wandering Kitty and asked, "Who found the Oregon Trail?"

As always, Wandering Kitty was ready with an answer. "Fur trappers called Mountain Men. They lived thousands of miles from civilization. Their only friends were the Native Americans. The mountain men's lives were hard and perilous. There were a lot of wild animals. To put it briefly, they ate anything that didn't eat them first."

The cats had seats on the boxes and bedding under the cover. It was fun for them to curl up on the bedding and look out from beneath the cover flaps. There was always something new to see. Their temporary owners were walking beside the wagon, and when Cynthia got tired she sat with the cats and asked lots of questions. Suddenly they heard, "Look, look, on the left side!" All eyes turned to see the Wind Wagon going out of control and crashing!

They all rushed over, along with a crowd of people. Thankfully, the Wind Wagon's occupants had jumped out just in the nick of time. They escaped serious injury and, other than a few bumps and bruises, were unscathed. But it showed all of them, human and feline alike, just how dangerous this trip could be.

23

After a few days of traveling, almost all of the pioneers realized they had overloaded their wagons. Now they were left with no choice: if they ever hoped to make it to their destination, it was necessary to lighten the load. They immediately started throwing things out. The trail was already littered with iron stoves, porcelain, mirrors, chamber pots, lanterns, schoolbooks, clocks, even furniture…and now the amount of junk was about to double in a matter of mere minutes.

Though the travelers had (many times) been advised not to overload their wagons, a large number of them had insisted on taking along some luxuries and items of sentimental value. Well, that turned out to be very bad planning on their part. It was sad for them indeed, but it lightened the load for their weary animals. Now they could make the rest of the trip without breaking their backs.

24

It was time for Rascal once again to record in his trusty diary all that was going on…

I'm now writing backwards. Three days ago…Tuesday morning…I began to write something here that I could not finish. Now I have enough time – plenty of time, in fact – because it is raining again. Splashing over the swampy ground was not too funny; though listening to the beat of the rain was fun. After a few more days on the trail, the migrants settled into a well-organized daily routine. Dear Diary, you will not imagine – we wake before sunup! Compared to our old place in Catanada where we slept sometimes until 10:00am! Feed animals, cook the breakfast, get horses to the wagons or yoke the oxen and hit the trail. We have a break for lunch and at 6:00pm we set the camp by circling the wagons. It is not for protection against Indians but the circle provides a purrrrfect corral for loose livestock.

Today when sleepy and cranky Sofia

woke up she said, "I'm going to wait for a train." My brother Philosopher, who reads lots of books, answered, "It looks like you did not learn the history of America well. You would have to wait until 1869, twenty more years, to be able to ride a train."

Wandering Kitty told us, that the farther we get from the Missouri River, the less swampy the ground will be. Before us lay a vast flat grassy plain. WESTWARD HO!!!!!

Meanwhile, the people became accustomed to the cats and did not bother them; they had their own problems. The cats were keeping an eye on the few dogs there, but they were somewhere behind the wagons with the oxen teams. Rascal smelled that some of them did not have very good intentions toward felines so 'better to be careful than sorry' he told the others. They all made sure that they stayed alert for the dogs, or, for that matter, any other dangers they might have to confront. There was no telling what they might encounter out there on the wild frontier.

As one day melted into the next, the flatlands were endless and the cats got bored. "What a monotonous routine we have – start at six, travel 'til 11, camp, rest and feed, start again at two, travel until six, camp for the night. What a boring life!" Sofia whined.

"We may be able to take a small walk later," advised Rascal, who was looking for something new and interesting to write in his diary.

25

One day after lunch, the sun chased the clouds away and it became bright and clear. The cats ran ahead of the wagons. The road lay before them, a single straight track, thick and high with grass. Something moving off to the side caught Sofia's eye. "Look!" she gasped, pointing in horror to the road ahead. The head of a snake lay in the grass on one side of the road and his tail on the other side. The rest of the cats only saw something quivering in the grass. The cats turned tail and ran as fast as they could back toward the wagons.

"What's the trouble?" asked Wandering Kitty, as the cats ran past him like a tornado.

"I saw a sssssnake," said Sofia, trembling. "It was longer than the road is wide."

Wandering Kitty laughed. "Seeing things a bit fancy. You'll get used to these little creatures soon."

"This was not little," she said indignantly. "If you wish I'll show you the place."

The cats reached the spot where the snake had been spotted. Wandering Kitty looked at the track for a moment, and then meowed softly, saying, "Sofia, you're right."

"I guess I don't really enjoy walking now," added Lumby and he jumped onto the wagon. The rest of the cats followed him. *I'm like a mini snack to this snake*, thought the black and white kitten.

As they slowly covered mile after mile, each day seemed to blend right into the next. *It would be easy to lose track of time out here*, Rascal thought. But at least he had the opportunity to write in his diary.

> *A week ago we crossed the Kansas River and today we are ready for another big crossing – the Independence Crossing of the Big Blue River. I like the idea of crossing before camping for the night because rain and storms could raise the water level and might detain us for several days. Actually as a cat I hate every crossing of any water but we have no choice, although crossing the Kansas River was not bad.*

Suddenly the wagon stopped and Rascal sprang up to find out why. Cynthia's father jumped down over the wheel. The whole wagon train moved slowly then stopped. The river was very swollen and people were forced to make camp before crossing. The guide of the wagon train said they were now only a few miles away from one of the most scenic and beautiful places along the trail, a camp called Alcove Spring.

The cats strolled up the small creek and found a large spring, as cold and pure as if it had just melted from ice. A beautiful cascade of water gushed from a ledge of rocks into a basin buried in a variety of shrubs and the cats found the name Alcove Springs engraved on the rocks and on the trunks of the trees surrounding it. They also saw pioneer names carved in the stones. All the women from the trail washed clothes. For them it was a good opportunity to do this necessary cleaning job. Mr. Isaac fished and caught a catfish three feet long. Cats love fish! Maybe having to cross this river was not going to be such a bad thing after all.

"It's a sunny day, nothing bad has happened, almost perfect harmony prevailed all day long and the catfish was very tasty," Rascal wrote in his diary.

After sunset a full moon appeared above the treetops to the west of camp. Tired but content, the cats, horses, mules and humans all went to sleep. But a little past midnight, a terrific thunderstorm roared over the camp. It raged and poured out its floods of water almost all night. If not for the protection of the bluffs against the wind from one side and the woods on the other, the tents would have been swept away by the storm. The sky was wrapped in a sheet of flame and deafening crashes of thunder cascaded one after another with ear-splitting peals. It seemed as if the end of the world had come. Rascal and the other cats had never witnessed such a storm before and it frightened them more than any of them cared to admit.

The morning, however, came clear, cloudless and peaceful. It seemed as if the world had returned to normal. The rain, however, had swollen the river again, causing it to rise even more, by several feet. It was a scary sight indeed.

And there was one other problem. Though the cats thought the Alcove Spring was certainly beautiful, the place was home to giant swarms of big, vicious, hungry mosquitoes that constantly bothered them. They heard people jokingly say to one another that the mosquitoes were so big they could be mistaken for turkeys. It was funny, but not so funny when you got bitten.

26

That night Rascal had a scary dream about rats. He woke up very nervous with lots of frightening images still in his head. He checked the bushes surrounding the camp, but found nothing suspicious. Throughout the next day, however, he thought and thought about his dream, though he did not tell the others about it. After all, why bother them with his problems? He saw that the other cats were very relaxed, taking sunbaths and waiting to cross the river. Oh, how he wished he could just lay back and enjoy himself too...but not with his mind still preoccupied by rats.

Sofia, too, had her own worries. She was still afraid of rattlesnakes and was sleeping in the wagon. The day was beautiful; the rich and luxuriant trees were lit by the bright sunshine and were alive with the songs of birds. Always curious, Rascal took a little walk alone into the woods.

On his way back, hungry and tired, he heard a faint cry for help. Without any caution he ran toward the voice, forgetting about snakes or other dangers lurking around every corner. There, on the old path lay a skinny, little, spotted, strange looking cat. His fur was yellowish red to grayish yellow with rows of large, dark rosettes and spots on his pale underside. His tail had black rings and a black tip. He had a slim head and round ears.

Suddenly, rain that fell with a heavy roar obscured the forest. Rascal only had time to cover the quivering and exhausted stranger with his own body.

"I don't like this weather," he meowed. "One moment we have sun and seconds later a thunderstorm," he murmured to himself, peering through the looming rain down the trail that led back to the camp.

When the storm stopped as abruptly as it had begun, the sun streamed through the clouds. Rascal was as wet as a catfish and pleaded, "Please help, anybody, please, cat fur is not agreeable to being wet and cats are not related to catfish."

27

Somebody heard him crying for help and soon there were footsteps headed his way. "Come to my fire," Rascal heard the pleasant voice of a stranger. He looked up, and there was a man standing there with clear dark eyes and an intelligent face, dressed in brown with a matching cowboy hat on his head. "First let's make a fire and dry you and your friend," said the human.

With surprising speed the man kindled a roaring fire, in spite of everything being so wet and soaked by the rain. Soon the warmth of the fire changed the wet cats into dry ones. Rascal looked around and saw the man take some powder, mix it with water and with the words, "This is pemmican (powdered dry meat)," gave the starved, skinny cat the drink. The cat licked a few drops of the dirty looking fluid, then opened his eyes and said, "Number Seven says thank you, sir."

Not only Rascal's tail, but his eyes were questions marks. What was happening here was indeed very strange.

"My name is Joking Horse, what's yours?" asked the stranger.

"Rascal," he said aloud, and thought, *I think only I have a normal name here.*

"So do you study mathematics?" questioned Joking Horse.

"What's that?" asked Number Seven in surprise.

"Do you have a family?" asked Rascal.

"No, they are all dead…the rats," mumbled Number Seven, and he started to cry.

"What rats?" asked Rascal, becoming frightened and tense.

"Rats…rats…rrrrats." Every time he murmured, he shook with fear.

Joking Horse covered the little spotted cat with a blanket and laid him close to the fire to sleep. Rascal was by now doing his best to act bravely, sharing his own adventures with the man, the ones he had had with rats not so long ago. He explained how, with the help of cows, horses and other cats, they had fought the rats and won the battle.

"That is a future story, in the year 1860," said Joking Horse, smiling and added, "I know, for you it is the past, for me too. I live in the 21st century in a beautiful country squeezed between two oceans."

28

"Catanada!" exclaimed Rascal, waking Number Seven up for a moment before he fell back asleep again. "What are you doing here!" This was even more bizarre than he could have imagined. This man was from the future? Then again, his story really was no more strange than what Rascal and his friends had been through, so why not? Still, what an amazing coincidence.

"The same thing you are doing. I'm a writer," the man calmly explained. "I'm working on a book about the Oregon Trail. When I need more information after reading all the diaries and old books, I close my eyes and imagine the place I want to be, then…I'm there, to learn more first hand, so I can write the history accurately. By the way, tonight, if you want to go with me, I have an appointment with a very interesting person."

The idea of writing down exact history was intriguing. In his own way, with his diaries, Rascal was doing the same thing. He never imagined he would have so much in common with a human being. Sometimes, just when he thought he had everything in life figured out, something new would happen that would change everything. This most assuredly seemed to be one of those times. As he was deep in thought, the man repeated his question. "Well, are you going to go with me?"

This time Rascal nodded in agreement. Then he looked at the sleeping cat next to him. "What about him?" he asked.

"Don't worry about Number Seven. I'll hide him in my wagon so the rats won't get him."

29

Rascal was curious and excited about the meeting. He helped Joking Horse to put Number Seven into a wooden box, covered for warmth. The exhausted kitten did not want to eat. He just wanted to keep sleeping and sleeping. And who could blame him after what he'd been through?

After supper when everybody else had gone to bed Rascal went to Joking Horse. Without exchanging a word they took a walk toward a small brook with no name. They sat on the log of a cottonwood tree. Rascal was purring with closed eyes. When he opened them, they were still sitting on the log, but near a wooden log cabin.

"He's not at home," whispered Joking Horse.

"Who?"

"The great Cherokee man."

They listened to the singing birds. After a while Rascal became impatient and asked, "Where is he now?"

"He's walking as usual in the woods with Ah-yo-ka, his daughter. They should be back soon," whispered Joking Horse, his eyes never leaving the small path partly covered with bushes of huckleberry.

"Who is he?" inquired the cat.

"Psssst, be quiet, somebody is coming. I hear human steps."

Rascal opened his eyes very wide, but nobody was there. The wind was low. No smell even reached his nose. He was utterly perplexed. Clearly, there was nobody there…at least not that he could see. How could this be? What super abilities could this human have that cats were lacking?

"Is he a ghost?" he asked, not entirely sure if he even believed in such things.

"No! He's real. We came back in time, so he's still alive. His name is Sequoyah – in the Cherokee language it means 'pig's foot'."

"That's not really a nice name," said Rascal.

"Maybe not, but now there are lots of parks and trees named after him. Sequoyah was crippled, but he had a dream that he could take each Cherokee word and write it down."

They sat quietly and listened to the forest. The birds' song stopped as it did before the thunderstorm. Something in the air was heavy and scary. Suddenly without any warning the log cabin was engulfed in flames. A few humans ran into the forest and disappeared. Rascal felt the fur on the top of his back stand up.

"They are Cherokee people! Why did they set fire to Sequoyah's cabin?" the man cried out.

"Now he'll think we did that," said Rascal, frightened and confused. "The fire is so big, there's no fire alarm or phone to call 911! What can we do?"

30

Just then Rascal saw a fire truck, a big noisy city, huge buildings around him and a cement parking lot full of cars. His will and desire to help was so strong that it had immediately transported him to the present, but in this exact same place. People surrounded the strange meowing cat, cars honked, traffic…

Panicking, he did not know what to do, when a soothing voice came from his new friend. "Rascal! Calm down. This isn't our fault. We have to wait for Sequoyah to help…Don't feel guilty." Then suddenly, Rascal was back again at the side of Joking Horse, not far from the remains of Sequoyah's burned up log cabin.

"Sequoyah spent most of his time working on the Cherokee alphabet," Joking Horse went on. "His home was filled with piles of strange symbols, which he named 'talking leaves'. Sequoyah was the first person in history to invent a written language alone. Alone! Can you imagine! He did this to help his people use the written language to write down the old stories. The alphabet could help the people understand each other better. Now, they've destroyed it all!"

This made Rascal intensely sad. He had always had nothing but the utmost respect and admiration for writers. Being an author himself (of his beloved diaries) he knew the power of the written word. In fact, he couldn't imagine what life must have been like before the invention of the written language. How boring!

"I wouldn't believe it if I hadn't seen it with my own eyes," meowed Rascal in a very melancholic way.

"Now you see that not all your own kind are friends and not all strangers are your enemies," said Joking Horse.

"That's right. We are not his family," Rascal replied. "But we do support him and we wish him the best! We writers have to stick together, you know."

"I know why they did that!" Joking Horse exclaimed. "They think he was making bad spells. The Indians remembered that the medicine men taught Sequoyah how to find the special herbs and roots they used to heal the sick."

Rascal perked up his ears. He heard a noise and very soon a man appeared on the path. He was on the short side and slightly lame. A small girl accompanied him. He wore the traditional shirt, leggings, moccasins, and turban. No introduction was necessary: the man was Sequoyah!

He did not seem to know any English, yet they seemed to have no problem understanding one another. Rascal listened while Joking Horse spoke with Sequoyah in a strange tongue. Rascal just stared at him, mesmerized by his presence. The small girl said something while looking at the burned cabin. Rascal did not understand words but he knew perfectly well what she was talking about. Incredible – he could not wait to record that in his diary.

Meantime, Sequoyah and Joking Horse took a large piece of buckskin and the Cherokee carefully wrote his alphabet on it, everything he had in his head. When he was finished, he turned to the burned cabin and said, "I know I must leave now. This is the second time fire has destroyed my writing. The first time my wife took all the pieces of bark which I'd penned the characters on. She threw them into the fire. Luckily, by then I had consigned the talking leaves to my memory, so I could reproduce them without much difficulty. Some people think I'm wasting my time, others are even saying that I've come under the spell of witchcraft or I'm insane. In spite of this, I will help my people to write and read."

With the words, "Now it is time for me to say goodbye," he and Ah-yo-ka left the sad place.

"Where are they going?" asked Rascal, wishing that they could stay.

"They'll travel to other territories. I know he'll succeed. I believe in his dream," said Joking Horse with a smile and sat down again on the cottonwood log..

31

"Please, tell me more about this small but big man!" said Rascal later, when they were approaching their camp. He was determined to find out all that he could. He was intensely curious, of course, and he knew his big brother Philosopher would have lots of questions too.

The man was more than happy to relate more to his feline friend. "Sequoyah built another cabin in the wilderness where he continued to work on his alphabet. It took him 12 years' work to complete it! The alphabet contains 86 symbols. When he'd finished, he returned east and showed it to the Tribal Council. It was the year 1821."

"May we go there at that time and see the happy faces of all those people?" asked, Rascal, now more ready than ever for another historical adventure.

The man had a broad smile now. "Yes, but first we have to check on Number Seven, then we can go quickly and come back before sunrise."

When they returned to the camp, the rescued kitty was still asleep. Rascal saw no need to disturb him and he took off with his new friend to the year 1821.

There, Sequoyah was showing the men of the Tribal Council his alphabet, but they thought it was a trick. They were very suspicious of the strange new thing and concerned about what kind of dark evil it might bring to them. Sequoyah was determined to teach them the truth.

"I want to prove that I'm not tricking you and I'll show that any Cherokee who speaks this language may learn to read and write it in five hours," he said proudly.

Most of the older men sat in a tight circle with their arms folded over their chests, wearing the grim faces of skeptics. But a young boy named Punch Head, filled with a youthful zest for learning new things, jumped up and volunteered to be the first to try.

"Okay, I would like to learn it; we shall all see with our own eyes and hear with our own ears whether or not this will truly work," he said.

When the youngster had learned the alphabet and found that it was fun, more curious young boys wanted to know what the talking leaves were saying. All of them were fascinated, and soon the older men, and some of the squaws, wanted to learn the strange new art.

"Sequoyah taught the system to three Cherokee youths who were able to learn it quickly and easily and the tribal leaders became enthusiastic. In just a short time Sequoyah became a hero, a genius. This led to the establishment of the Cherokee Phoenix, the first newspaper published by American Indians," Joking Horse told Rascal, while looking at Sequoyah with astonishment.

"What an example of courage and patience!" added Rascal with admiration. "I wish to have such patience." He felt honored to witness such a heroic genius from the past. *It's one thing to read about such people,* he thought, *it's quite another to actually see them in action.*

Soon after Rascal and Joking Horse returned to the camp for a well-deserved evening of peaceful slumber.

32

"Wake up, Rascal!" Sofia whispered, nudging him. "It's time for breakfast."

"Sofia! You wouldn't believe the incredible things I've seen! I personally met Sequoyah, the inventor of writing!"

"Rascal!" exclaimed Snow, "You know who invented writing? It was me as a Seshat in Ancient Egypt. Don't you remember our trip to Ancient Egypt?"

All of them laughed heartily. Sofia, Snow and the rest of the cats did not believe Rascal had really had such an adventure. They said it was a dream or just his imagination, and none of them took seriously what he was saying.

Rascal, however, was not about to give up so easily. "I'll prove it to you if you want," he insisted. "I learned how to go to another place in another time to learn more about history. We don't need to go to the Enchanted Forest looking for Samuel the Prehistoric Cat to help us do that. We don't need heavy and strange marked doors to other worlds. I've found a much simpler way."

So that afternoon Rascal took his friends to the same cottonwood log near the brook without a name and told them to imagine where they wanted to go. He explained to them that their intent must be for a good purpose only, otherwise the magic would not work. The cats agreed to do as they were told, and they were ready to see Sequoyah, but Rascal's magic did not work. They were sitting on the log; Lumby fell down. Mosquitoes were biting them badly. This was turning out to be the exact opposite of what Rascal had hoped for.

"Don't give up, let's try again," said Rascal, encouragingly, but his new skill did not work no matter how hard he tried. The cats returned to the wagons joking about Rascal and his historical travels. They did not believe the story about the rescued cat either.

"Rascal! I know you've had some crazy ideas but this is the worst one ever," chided Sofia.

"Don't worry, Sofia, I'll explain to you slowly. Besides, I have one more secret," said Rascal. He then told her about the writer from Catanada who was also on the Oregon Trail on this same wagon train trip.

The cats listened to his new information without any enthusiasm because they did not believe it. They just smiled and made lots of jokes about his rich imagination.

The next day, as the water was still high, the pioneers constructed a crude ferry-boat and named it a Blue River Rover. First they made dugouts of large cottonwood trees. Two of these they framed together, so that the wheels of the wagons rested in the canoes. Lines were attached to both ends and the raft was pulled back and forth by hand and finally the wagons, horses and mules were safely landed on the west bank.

"We are now in a 'howling wilderness,' except for the old wagon-road we are traveling on," said a friendly voice. Rascal jumped from the wagon and much to his delighted surprise there Joking Horse was standing.

"How is the kitty we rescued?" asked Rascal.

The man's face looked solemn and grim. "Number Seven is very sick. He has a fever. I don't know if he'll survive. He looks like all of his nine lives have expired."

"No! He must live!" cried Rascal, distraught at the bad news. His sensitive nose sniffed the air. "I smell some mystery...mystery about rats! You would not believe, Joking Horse, what we had in 1860 with rats. We almost all got killed! I'm going to purr until Number Seven gets healthy," he promised.

33

Day by day, both cats and humans, with lots of toil, were moving their destiny to the place they chose, though it seemed to be at the other end of the world. Undaunted, mile after mile they pushed ahead.

Rascal stayed by Joking Horse and the sick kitten. His cat friends spent all day sleeping or walking slowly close to the wagon with Cynthia and Lou. Rascal learned a lot from the writer, who proved to know not only how to keep his readers entertained, but also how to make a fire without matches, how to cook without pots, which plants were edible and which were to be avoided. Slowly Number Seven felt better but he still did not talk about his problems. He just sat and looked without seeing and listened without hearing. They asked him all kind of questions, but it was difficult to get any information from him. Rascal was not only curious, but also afraid that something was not right...

One afternoon Joking Horse said to Rascal. "We are now 310 miles out of Independence. We are in the place where we say goodbye to the Little Blue River.

Our trail will now jump up onto the Platte River and continue west along the riverbank."

Rascal ran to share this news with the other cats.

They greeted the Platte River with mixed emotions. "This broad and shallow river is a mile wide and doesn't look like a river at all," Sofia complained.

As it turned out, she was not the only one who was less than thrilled with their circumstances. Some farmer spoke in a loud voice to a group of people. "This river is too thick to drink and too thin to plow."

"It isn't a river, it's moving sand," Snow criticized and her husband Dandy added, "It's only an inch deep."

That evening Wandering Kitty said, "I'd like to be a guide and bring more kittens to the West."

"Great idea! You should write something about it!" replied Rascal.

"I'll write tomorrow," he said, inspired by Rascal's words of encouragement.

"Don't wait until tomorrow because tomorrow never comes."

"Today I'm tired, but tomorrow I'll have more time and I'll be ready. I'd like to write everything about the Wild West. If I could write just one book to help other cats understand the race to the West, I'd be happy. Yep! Tomorrow for sure I'll start the book," said Wandering Kitty.

The next day, which was the end of May, the wagon train reached Fort Kearney. The fort was the first military station built to protect Oregon Trail migrants.

Wandering Kitty said again, "I have to write about it tomorrow."

After traveling 18 miles, the pioneers made camp. Before night Rascal suddenly jumped up and whispered to his friends, "Pinch my tail or I'm dreaming. When I took a walk as usual to check around, I saw a small camp fire behind our trail. It looks like somebody is secretly following us. A friend would not follow secretly!"

"Holy Cats! We have to defend the humans and animals. They are our friends. What shall we do?" asked Snow.

Rascal looked each one straight in the eyes.

"Under darkness of night, let's sneak out and see. Be ready, guys, to take action."

34

With those words the cats left camp unnoticed. What they saw surprised them. To the windward side, near a small fire, were the dusky forms of some 25 rats, some standing, others half-reclining or quietly extended at full length upon the ground. The cats hid themselves behind a rock and with their good eyes they began to survey the surroundings. Far from the fire some murky figures were laying in a row.

"More rats I guess, but who are they?" whispered Rascal into Wandering Kitty's right ear. "Are they hostile or friendly? Why are they following the Oregon Trail?"

The cats moved with extreme caution through the dark night. With limbs shivering and teeth chattering they stood their ground, waiting until all the rats went to sleep. The rats were trying to impress one another with tall tales of their many experiences. One was telling how he chased a deer for a week without stopping to eat or sleep. Another spoke of riding a grizzly bear full tilt. One of them claimed that he had danced with buffalo all day, then paddled up the Mississippi

River in a canoe made of stone. There was no end to their stories. Finally one by one they got up and with squeaks, click sounds and whines, accompanied by the crack of a whip, they harnessed strange looking cats and hitched them to the wagons. Rascal's and his friends' patience was tested to the utmost. What they'd discovered shocking. Rats were everywhere and they had cats to pull their little wagons!

"They travel at night," said Wandering Kitty in amazement.

"They are sneaky animals," whispered Rascal, angered and stunned.

Still laying behind the rock, looking down, the cats had to decide what to do. "Kill them," growled Wandering Kitty.

"Let's talk," decided Rascal, then he shouted, "Stop! Where are you going, rats?"

"Who's there?" answered a few rat voices. Rats have a keen sense of hearing, but have poor vision.

Rascal boldly went closer to the first wagon pulled by four little spotted cats. The captain of the trail, a huge brown rat named Whip Cracker jumped from the wagon and with a whip in his right paw he came closer to Rascal. "What's your business here?"

"We never saw cats pulling a wagon before," answered Philosopher, standing close to his brother. "That's all."

The rat turned around and shouted, "Muddy! Frosty! Come here and explain to these greenhorns."

A most unusual cat first approached, slowly. He

had a long narrow head, a flattened forehead, large eyes, and small ears. He was a little bigger than Rascal but had a short tail and short legs. His claws made a noise on the rocky road since they were not fully retracted into their protective sheaths.

"I'm Muddy, the Flat Head Cat" he introduced himself, showing all his pointed and backward facing teeth. A thick reddish-brown coat with a silvery tinge covered the skinny body of the tired animal. Behind him trotted another strange, stocky- built cat with a flattened face. He had long, sandy fur with a white tip, producing a frosty appearance. He had black spots on his head, a few black stripes on his back and more black stripes on his tail, long whiskers and a white chin.

Muddy continued. "We are owned by our Master."

"This is the first time I've ever seen rats that out-smarted cats," meowed Rascal.

"How we can help you?" asked Wandering Kitty, ready for any action.

"We don't need your help, the rats are helping us. Otherwise we may become food for coyotes or wolves. The rats feed us…"

Rascal interrupted impatiently. "What happens if one of you gets sick?"

"The rats send us to the best hospital where we get good care."

"Hospitals in the wilderness?" asked Wandering Kitty.

"Yes, the rats know everything and we trust them completely."

"What if the rats desert a sick cat on the path, leaving it as food for coyotes?"

"No! The rats wouldn't do that, they care for us," Muddy replied indignantly.

Rascal and his friends shook their heads sadly.

"Now! Muddy! Frosty! Get to work!" called an angry voice.

"We must go. One last suggestion. Don't come here, our masters don't like it. They live by the strong law of penalties and pains."

"We don't want more pains," added Frosty sadly.

When Flat Head Cat and Flat Face Cat left, Rascal asked his friends, "What can we do? Those poor cats are blindly following rats."

His brother Philosopher answered, "Right now, nothing, but tonight we'll take counsel and try to find the best way."

The cats watched as a strange train passed by with black rats, brown rats and a few families of pack rats driving west. Behind the last wagon, tangled in ropes with the rope around his neck, a small black kitten stumbled.

"Stop! Wait!" shouted Rascal.

35

The pack rat answered immediately. "He's our prisoner. He's the worst bandit. He's robbed stagecoaches, banks and us rats. We're going to hang him up somewhere on the way."

"I'll buy him as my slave," retorted Rascal. "How much do you want for the skinny tinny worth-nothing kitten?"

"Twenty potatoes."

"Okay!" agreed Rascal.

"Twenty juicy crusty potatoes," repeated the rat.

While Philosopher, Dandy, Snow and Sofia ran back to the camp for potatoes, Rascal asked more questions about how the rats treated their slaves.

The pack rat named Pokey took the end of the rope and approached Rascal. "He may look small but he's a devil. He bit off the tip of my tail and his sharp claws left ugly marks on my brother's back."

The black kitten, who had one white whisker on the left side of his face and big yellow round eyes stood quietly while Pokey was explaining. "Maybe he'll grow up to be a good tamed cat after all. You just need to treat him well. I mean, 15 whips every morning, 10 whips at noon and five before sleep. If you don't know why, he'll know why, for sure."

Pokey looked up and saw Sofia, Snow, Dandy and Philosopher returning with a sack full of potatoes. They handed the sack over and "Westward Ho!" Pokey squeaked simultaneously with the crack of the whip and the train moved off.

"Ouch! Our brothers and sisters must suffer," said the black kitten, looking after the last wagon as it disappeared.

"Let's take those ropes off of you, my friend," meowed Rascal in a friendly voice.

"My name is Onyx. I'm a free cat, not a slave. Those rats wanted to brainwash me, but it was in vain," he said, smiling sadly. "Thank you, guys, I will do everything to pay you back for your 20 potatoes."

"Don't worry, our human friends have lots of potatoes," said Rascal with a rascally laugh. "They bought them for a good price at the last stop, Fort Kearney, and if not for us, the mice would've eaten them all, so we are set."

Lumby approached the kitty. "You're younger than me! I'm a teenager now and you're still a small kitten." He smiled and gave him a friendly lick on his nose.

"You must be hungry," added Sofia. "Let's go home. I mean, to our camp."

36

A few days passed, Onyx became more energetic and Number Seven began to look healthier.

Rascal told everyone that he had a strange dream every night about the enslaved cats needing their help.

"Let's call our Prehistoric Cat Samuel from the Enchanted Forest to help us fight," a voice piped up.

"No, he is busy teaching other cats. By the way he has already told us: fight without fight, using power instead of force. By purring we can win!" said Rascal.

"We can overcome all enemies by purring; the rats will get lost," a few more voices cried.

"That seems too easy to be true," said Wandering Kitty.

"Let's discuss it," said Philosopher.

The cats found a quiet place among the stones and sage bushes and started thinking what to do.

"Get the humans to help us, they can use traps for rats, the farmers have always done that" advised Wandering Kitty, "The best way is to give rats poison and kill the ratstards! I prefer to kill them all!" His voice dripped with anger.

"No! Our history is full of killing and fighting, now we've learned another way, much better and easier," gasped Rascal.

"Yep, right!" said Wandering Kitty scornfully. "I'm ready to fight and even die."

"One of the main tools we have is intention," announced Philosopher, sounding calm and reasonable as always. "Our intention is to help the cats, that's all, but the problem is – how?"

Hour passed by hour and still the cats talked. Finally, with no clear idea what to do, they decided to just go and scout and learn more about the rats and the possibilities of outsmarting them. They all agreed that, lacking any other sort of plan, this would be the wisest strategy, at least for now. Sofia stayed at the camp with Onyx, Number Seven, and Wandering Kitty, who announced that in case of problems he would come and rescue them. Lumby, though still a kitten, was the champion in purring and he had the best eyes to see far. He also had his experience from Ancient Egypt and Medieval Europe to draw on.

The sun was up when the small group silently set out to look for the rats' camp. It was farther than they had remembered from before. It seemed that the rats were taking a more northwest direction and the Oregon Trail went straight to the west.

"It looks like the trails separate," whispered Rascal.

"Soon there will be two separate trails to Oregon," meowed Lumby. He was confused.

"Don't forget what Wandering Kitty told us.

'When you find yourselves in trouble just give a holler!'" reminded Bunny, then his words dropped to a whisper. "Something is behind us."

They all spun around but it was too late! Suddenly, a net covered all of them and the laughing voices of rats burst out.

"We're trapped!" they all cried.

"We told you they're greenhorns and know nothing about the Wild West, where only the strongest and smartest survive," laughed the rats.

The cats, now all tangled in the ropes, were being walked slowly towards the rats' camp. Slave cats were sleeping on the hard ground in rows. They opened their eyes but closed them again without any excitement. They were too tired to have any feelings. The rats tied Rascal's and his friends' paws and put them into a wooden cage. Then they went to sleep. For them it was time of rest even though the sun was still high in the sky. The rats traveled at night.

The rats started snoring loudly. Rascal was thinking about how to escape. He whispered to his brother, "First of all don't fight, we have to purr and do the best we can, as Samuel taught us."

"What if they make us their slaves?" asked Bunny.

"Be quiet. I have to talk in my thoughts to Prehistoric Cat Samuel," said Rascal, and closed his eyes trying to communicate with his teacher. Soon he got an answer. *Do your best and purr as much as you can.*

"Tell our teacher that I want to go home," whispered Snow.

Rascal got Samuel's answer. *"You'll get home when your lesson is learned. For now you have to finish the Oregon Trail and maybe something else. Be brave, it was your own will to be there, to see the Wild West, I cannot change that for you."*

Rascal looked around. "Don't cry, Snow, it looks like we have to keep going with the mistakes we make and learn from them. There is always a solution to every problem. We can start by changing the way we feel about our situation"

"Let's try to do the best we can," Dandy said, gently touching his wife and acknowledging that Rascal was right.

"Yep, be the best slaves in the world," said Rascal sadly and started to purr. The rest of the cats followed him.

37

One hour after sunset the rats made breakfast, this time without fire. They distributed corn bread and water and a few bugs for the cats; they knew that cats were meat eaters and would not survive long on corn. Then they quickly got everything ready for the trip.

Rascal and his friends were tied up behind the wagon of the captain, Whip Cracker. Flat head cats, flat face cats and little spotted cats pulled the wagons. Every rat was nervous and in haste.

"Something is in the air," Rascal said in a whisper. "I smell danger. The rats are almost killing those cats with overwork."

"I don't see anything or smell anything, except maybe the nice smell of a camp fire," meowed Lumby.

Rascal answered, "That's not a fire from camp, it's the prairies on fire! The day before the rats caught us I noticed dense smoke at a distance behind us. I wasn't worried because the wind was blowing in the opposite direction."

"Quick! Catch up! Catch up!" screamed the panicked rats. "The wind has changed!"

They all ran for their lives, even the small rats and kittens. No one was riding a wagon: it was faster that way, as relieved wagons were pulled easier by the slave cats.

Flames were rapidly threatening to engulf them, lighting the sky and prairie, transforming the darkness of night into a bright day. It was an ocean of flames dancing with a mad fiery fury racing forward with the wind, leaving blackened destruction in its wake.

"How sudden and dreadful!" someone shouted. "What about our human and animal friends on the Oregon Trail? Are they still alive...Onyx, Sofia?" The cats were asking each other a million questions, running behind the wagon, pushing it sometimes to ease the spotted cats' burden. They had no choice, as they were tied up.

"Don't worry about them, the wind is going in our direction not towards them, we go more to north-west."

All of them ran at full speed with as much effort as never before. For a while the pursuing enemy kept even pace with rats and cats and at some points even threatened to overtake them.

"Run! Quick! Catch up! Catch up!" They squirmed and meowed, shouting until the fire changed direction with a strong wind pushing toward the east. Both rats and cats were in the same situation – they were alive one minute but they all might be dead the next.

Black rats, brown rats and pack rats were looking for their families as in a fitful panic some of them ran too fast ahead. Rascal watched with amazement as the huge Brown Rat Family embraced their kids and spoke to them with soft squeaks.

But the famished slave cats could not run for ever. Eventually wagons pulled by tired cats came to a stop. All of the animals were breathing very hard.

With great curiosity, Rascal looked at the animals with pointed noses and hairless feet and tails. Only pack rats had bushy tails.

Everybody took a rest and each cat was given a small piece of dried fish by the rats, who knew it was better to treat their pulling animals to food to sustain them than to have to pull the wagons themselves.

After midnight they made a few more miles and before sunrise they hid among the sagebrush and rocks and pitched camp.

38

Whip Cracker announced that after lunch he would start 'taming' the new cats to be the pulling animals for his wagon. He said, "They look strong and healthy and will do a great pulling job. They just need a few whips of encouragement."

Rascal was purring all the time hoping for a miracle rescue but the rats were preparing a cruel and fast training regime for the newcomers.

Before the 'training hour' struck Rascal said, "Remember to purr to the purrrfectness and be purrrfect all the time, even if we have be the most perfect slaves in the world. It's our own fault that we are where we are, that we are in training as slaves instead of staying safely at home sleeping so, eat and purr."

First Frosty and Muddy harnessed Rascal. Then Whip Cracker, with his whip in his right paw forced him to run in circles. Rascal was wearing the harness but was without a bit in his mouth. Cats have no break among the teeth where horses have and where the bit lies.

"Yes, that's right," squeaked Knucklehead, a black rat. "We have to teach them fast. Learning on the lunge is one of the best ways to acquire the best pulling cats in the world."

"Lunging is a tiring and time consuming operation, so let's do it faster than usual," Whip Cracker told Knucklehead.

Soon all of the newcomers were harnessed and running in circles.

"This is Western America's most unique vacation," whispered Rascal with a smile, when he passed close to his brother Philosopher, who failed to see the humor in his remark.

When the cats were really tired, the rats decided that it was time to start pulling the wagons. The rats' aggressive mood changed, as they were tired too. Maybe all of that purring was making its way into the rats' hearts...

39

At supper, just before sunrise, the rats decided that the cats needed more training in submission to masters. They discussed the best ways to bully the cats, as they usually had done with other slaves. They wanted to control the mass behavior of all cats. Slave masters would carefully educate and train them all to be ideal slaves.

Knucklehead turned to Whip Cracker as they sat near the small campfire eating baked potatoes. They talked about the best steps for molding the character of slaves.

"Strict discipline is very important," advised the captain.

"It's also very important for the cats to believe that their masters are superior," squeaked the black rat.

"Acceptance of the masters' standards and a deep sense of their own helplessness and dependence," added another black rat, named Rattus, "is vital to our success."

"Now we have to develop in these newcomers a sense of their own inferiority," pointed out a pack rat called Trade Rat.

Rascal and his friends were listening to everything the rats were saying and they knew that they must be strong and never give up their own self-esteem. "Guys, we must be strong," whispered Rascal to his friends. "Now is the time to show them our strong culture. We will never give up."

"Yes, we'll show them who will prevail," said Philosopher with a smile.

Bunny added, "After our experiences we should be strong enough already. If they laugh because I have no tail, I'll just smile into their whiskers and tell them the truth. I have no tail, so what? Not every animal has a tail. Humans have no tail and they are on the top of the ladder."

"Truth is the best defense against the bullies," meowed Philosopher and Rascal nodded.

Lumby turned his head to them and asked, "What does 'slave' mean? I don't understand. This morning I heard one pack rat tell all the cats that their offspring will be declared to be absolute slaves. What does that mean?" His young eyes were full of questions.

Bunny tried to explain to him. "A slave is a mercantile and movable property. And, as property they can't own anything. When cats are owned by rats and live to serve them without pay, that means they are slaves. Even their kittens are the property of the rats and they are usually the ones raising them, not their parents or grandparents. It's very sad."

"But where do the slaves come from?" Lumby

asked.

"Rats buy them at the slave auction," came the answer.

"Like we buy toys at the supermarket?"

"Quiet! It's time for sleep!" shouted one of the black rats.

40

Later, when all of the rats were snoring deeply, the cats resumed their discussion.

"How do slaves become slaves?" Rascal asked a cat named Friday 13 who was lying down nearby.

"By many bad and ugly ways, like for example, by fraud – the captains of ships invite cats on board and then carry them off. Or they come at night without any noise, surround a lonely family of cats and carry them away. Sometimes by force: rats will land, seize as many cats as they find and transport them away to one of their rat villages. The vessel I was in, we were kept on deck day and night, where the sails and a thin tarpaulin were our only protection from the sun and from bad weather. At meal times, in order to prevent greediness (so they told us), one rat would signal when we could all take the food and when we could eat it."

"They were giving the poor, unfortunate cats their first lesson in how to be submissive, I would guess," said Dandy.

Friday 13 continued the sad saga of slavery. "The

second mate and boatswain were really bad to us. When it was time to sleep they held a whip in their paws and shouted terrible things. Then they arranged us in different places for the night. The cats on the right side of the vessel were facing forward. Hmm, those on the left …with their faces towards the stern. Each of us had to lay on our right side. The rats considered that position to be preferable for the action of our hearts."

"Rats have no heart!" added a flat head cat, joining the discussion.

"I know," said Friday 13 with a nod. Then he tried to finish his somber story. "The smaller and younger cats were lodged near the bow. The biggest ones were selected for the greatest breadth of the vessel."

"Opossum! Why?" murmured Dandy.

"A worse hell started when the ship arrived at the destination port. They separated us out to the plantations of several masters…those rattstards! To see my family no longer…" The cat was meowing with tears now.

"It's the worst thing that can happen to a cat. To be banished from his own country, friends and family for ever…and to be made into beasts of burden."

Rascal and his friends were listening intently. This was almost too awful to believe.

"On the plantation, our sleep was very short, our labor continual and beyond our strength. Before we could go to sleep, we were forced to collect herbs and fuel for our master's family. So it was often past midnight when we finally went to our quarters. We ate something fast and if we were not in the fields early in the morning we would feel the lash on our backs. Bambara, Limba, Kru, Ashante and Brong. Where they are now? We worked together, they were my friends, and now we are here going west and they stayed behind on the wheat and corn plantation"

Soon dreams of freedom came to all of them as they slept.

41

Meanwhile, nervous Sofia, with Onyx, Number Seven and Wandering Kitty, were in the covered wagon rumbling along the dusty trail listening to the grinding and crunching of the steel-rimmed wooden wheels. The steady plodding of horses' hooves were added to the same melody every day.

We are going to die along this wild and lonely trail, Sofia was thinking, her face morose. It was the second day without Rascal, Philosopher, Bunny, Snow and Dandy. Sofia had a feeling that something horrible must have happened to her friends. Number Seven still felt his fear of the rats and he missed Joking Horse, who had also been gone now for a few days.

"What's the matter with you, Sofia?" meowed Onyx.

"I have to go to find my friends but I'm scared to go alone and I don't know where to go and in which direction to look for them."

"You are not alone, I'll go with you," purred Onyx, "and I'm the best scout on the prairie."

"I'm going too," insisted Wandering Kitty, with

a resolute face.

"Me too," said Number Seven. "Even though my human friend Joking Horse is far away, I'm ready to go and fight those rats."

"Where is Joking Horse?" asked Sofia, hoping that a human could be helpful.

"He went to visit another famous fixture of Western America's history, Sacagawea. But he'll be back soon, I hope."

"Who is Sacagawea?" asked Sofia curiously. She knew lots of Greek and Roman history, but not much about the Wild West.

"Sacagawea means Bird Woman. She carried her infant on a cradleboard with the Lewis and Clark expedition and so the baby, called Little Pomp, was the first and youngest explorer of the West..."

They all wanted to hear the story, but there was not enough time.

"You can read about it in the history books, but right now let's go and find our friends," said Wandering Kitty, reminding all of them of how serious the situation was.

And with those words the cats left the trail to look for Rascal and the rest.

After an hour of hot running they still had not located Rascal, or the rats or the small wagons pulled by slave cats. The weather was hot and sunny. The cats grew tired and still they could not find one trace of their friends, alive or dead.

"Not even a hairball," meowed disappointed Onyx.

42

Rascal realized that it was very difficult teaching purring to the slave cats. They had been bred on many lies, being told they were stupid, ugly, unworthy and incapable of doing anything without the rats. From the rats' point of view they needed endless fixing and correction.

That afternoon the cats heard a few of the rats shouting from behind, "Stop! Stop the wagons! We need help!"

Every wagon stopped and the other rats ran to see what had happened at the back of the trail. They found a wagon with a bare wheel. The wood had shrunk and the metal rim had fallen off.

"Nothing important, they just got a flat tire," Rascal said with a smile. And then he realized that the rats did not know what to do.

"Should we tell them?" asked Dandy.

"No, we'd better not. Do you want to slave all the way to Oregon?" replied Rascal.

Lumby quickly added, "But we don't want to lie to them, right Rascal? Bunny always teaches me to tell the truth."

Rascal said to one rat, "It's very easy to repair a flat tire – just put the wheel into water for a little while."

The rats were panicking and the slave cats realized that their bullies were not as strong and wise as they liked to be seen. They weren't even smart enough to listen to what Rascal had told them.

"All actions have consequences," purred Rascal with closed eyes. Suddenly he had a strange feeling, of somebody watching him closely. He looked with half open eyes and, without changing his position, he spotted, hidden behind a rock, a gray-blue cat with short fur and yellow eyes carefully watching him. Though he'd never seen this cat before, there was something familiar about him. The yellow eyes stared at him for a while, then they disappeared as the cat dived back into the bushes.

Dandy and Snow came to Rascal with some news. "There's a spy in this group. We saw him and we can smell that it's only one cat and he is not afraid of rats. His color is grayish blue, with yellow eyes."

"I saw those eyes!" Rascal exclaimed. "No fear! That's right! Those same eyes … if he's a spy so is Onyx! We must help Sofia, Wandering Kitty and the others. But how to warn them?"

43

At the same time, Onyx was telling Sofia that they needed to go even further away from the camp, otherwise they might not find their friends.

"You are young, how can we believe you?" asked Wandering Kitty

"I've known rats since the day I was born," answered Onyx. "Besides...eh, never mind...let's run fast."

They ran with all their strength and dedication to find their friends.

Two hours later Onyx began to recognize the long tracks of wooden wheels.

"They go in this direction," he called out, pointing excitedly toward north-west.

"They've either lost their way or the rats are up to something!" shrieked Sofia, as she looked nervously at the setting sun.

"We should go back to our camp before night. Tomorrow we can look for them again," advised Wandering Kitty.

"That's right, before night," agreed Number Seven.

Sofia sat looking back and forth. She was ready to

go back to camp, but she also wanted to keep looking. She did not know what to do. She wanted to fight her fears and be brave enough to press on into the night.

Onyx approached her and meowed, "Okay let's go to look for the rats, I can smell that they are not too far away."

Bravely, Sofia replied, "Yes, let's continue searching." Her love for her friends and her concern for their safety was a much more powerful force than her fear. Her courage pushed aside her anxiety and deep down inside she mustered up the courage that had lain there dormant.

All of the cats ran behind Onyx until the sun went down. Now it was too far and too late to go back to the camp, so they found some trees they could climb into to get some safe night sleep.

While Sofia and her group were falling asleep, Rascal and his band were just waking up.

44

After sunset the rats and their slave cats were waking up.

"Back to work..." sighed Dandy.

"I miss my home like never before. I will treasure every minute there if we ever get back," moaned Snow.

Lumby looked still very tired. "Meow! Me too! I miss my scratching post and playing with kitty toys."

Rascal slowly turned around. "I miss my catnip," he said.

Philosopher added, "I like to be petted not whipped. Petted by a human hand, not by a bull-skin whip"

"I think we're in buffalo country now," Rascal informed them.

He was right and the buffalo-tramped earth had dried into sharp points that pierced the soles of the cats' feet. They had to haul with all their strength. Reaching an unknown small river, they rested and prepared to ford the waterway. Rascal didn't like cold water and Philosopher tried to tell Whip Cracker about his brother's allergy to it, but the cruel rat only smiled a wicked smile and said, "With the help of my whip your brother will be cured from any allergy."

Another rat squeaked, "All of our hauling cats have forded the creeks and rivers until now without any problems."

The whip cracked, rats shouted and the cats quickly went into the water. Rascal's paws moved so fast that he began to pull the others. Suddenly his paws gave way. The rats seated in the wagon started to go under. With a good share of luck a few swimming cats, those with flat heads, were on the loose and immediately started a rescue action. They swam under water and with their sharp teeth they cut the harnesses and the wagon sank to the bottom while they returned to the surface. A few of them pulled Rascal by the tail and ears and dragged him out.

"That was a close call, brother," said Philosopher with tears, as he embraced Rascal.

The rats decided to pitch camp to rest and to dry off their wagons. They discovered that water indeed helped the wheels and the metal rims were now firmly settled on the wooden wheels. They happily squeaked and started to sink some of the wheels in the river. They now believed that water would help "cure" flat tires and prevent further flats in the future.

It was a night off for everybody, so the rats went around looking for fresh food and to get some exercise.

The night was clear and fresh. The slave cats who had rescued Rascal felt good. For the first time in their lives they experienced a feeling of accomplishment. Helping others was rewarding – they even started to purr. And the more they purred, the happier they became. The miracle of purring was passed from one cat to another all over the camp. Rascal, who knew the power of purring well, was observing it all with great joy.

"Our intention is to free the cats, not to add more slaves for the rats," Dandy muttered in happy tones.

"That's why we are here, because of our intention to free them and the best way to do that is from inside the enemy camp," explained Rascal, adding, "Soon something may happen, something advantageous and positive to all of us."

Philosopher nodded emphatically. "That's exactly what I felt today."

Lumby was playing "buffalo pie frisbee" with a young little spotted cat. Then he found a huge, round, dark hairball. It was a perfectly round ball, about two inches in diameter. Such a ball was a great find, because cats' hairballs are usually small and long not round, they are more like the middle finger of a human.

As the sun rose the next morning, before going to sleep the cats looked across the meadow and saw an amazing sight. There was a moving mass on the horizon: frightful droves, as far as the eye could see. The ground seemed to be moving. Hundreds of thousands of buffalos were causing this illusion!

As the rats turned to sleep, suddenly somebody

yelled, "Danger!"

Everybody looked up. A gray, shaggy blur was moving down the hill. The large herd of buffalo was galloping towards them at incredible speed. The cats and rats ran for cover. They hid among the rocks as quickly as they could. Rascal was thinking about his friends but he saw only buffalo hooves silhouetted against the blue sky. The ground was shaking more than ever! A swathe of dirty fur and deafening noise roared up to the small wagons and trampled them all flat. The buffalo charged right through the camp. The stampede seemed to last forever.

45

Sofia, Onyx, Number Seven and Wandering Kitty were still sleeping in the tree when they heard and saw the stampede passing not too far away. They waited for it to pass and worried about the other cats and their human friends. The huge herd was thundering toward them from both sides. This was their first encounter with a great western legend – the dangerous and frightening buffalo.

46

With the disappearance of the last buffalo, the panic-stricken cats and rats looked around. They were thankful, that none of them was dead but the rats had lost their wagons and everything that was carried in them.

Suddenly a strong cat voice came from the bushes. "Ruined rotten rats! Or is that ratten?" Everyone looked round with surprise. It was the gray cat with yellow eyes. He was alone. Looking straight into the eyes of the captain of the rats, he said, "All animals are equal! It doesn't matter if they have naked tails or hairy ones, whether they meow or squeak, we are all living creatures and shouldn't be slaves to each other. Your cruel way of life must be ended now!"

Everyone was stunned. The rats without whips lost their confidence. The cats noticed that immediately. They seized the moment to help the lone stranger. Lumby started to purr first, then Rascal and the other cats. Soon all cats – swimming cats, little spotted cats, flat head cats and flat face cats – were all purring. The rats started backing up, their fear increasing with each step. Somebody gave a command

and the cats dashed boldly toward the terrified rats who were now fleeing away like lightning. Nobody had ever seen anything like it before.

"Tyrants are always cowards!" meowed Rascal.

"We are free! Unbelievable! Our dream has come true at last!" yelled joyful cats and frightened rats did not stop running until they were lost from view.

The strange cat with yellow eyes walked over to Rascal and introduced himself. "My name is Grey Dust. I came here to rescue Onyx, my son. The rats wanted to hang him up, so I was sneaking around to help him. Then I saw you save his life by paying those rattstards 20 potatoes. I will give you back whatever you wish for rescuing my only son.

"We have to go back, because our brothers in the east are still enslaved, working on wheat and corn plantations for the rats. We've learned how to free them by the power of purring," said Frosty.

"That's right! By purring you will change the energy surrounding the rats and they have to learn to respect all animals as their own," said Rascal.

"My brother speaks the truth!" said Philosopher with a nod and Lumby danced the dance of freedom. The younger cats joined him. For them, it was the first time they had ever tasted freedom in their young lives and there was indeed much to celebrate.

The rest of the cats soon decided to travel east to rescue all their enslaved brothers. Grey Dust was anxious to find his son, Onyx, the black kitten. Rascal, Philosopher, Snow, Dandy and Bunny were happy to go back to their own friends.

Bunny smelled around and asked, "Why is the smell of urine so strong from some of the wagons?"

Philosopher explained: "The wagons belonged to pack rats. Usually they build nests in the base of a prickly pear tree or in caves, but while traveling to Oregon they built nests in their wagons. The filthy nests are called 'middens'. The middens are normally built out of sticks, but sometimes they will use plant fragments and animal dung. Then the pack rat urinates in the midden during the time it lives there."

Bunny wrinkled up his nose in disgust. "Yuuuuk! Why?"

"Some substances in the urine crystallize as it dries out, cementing the midden together," explained Grey Dust, sounding like a schoolteacher.

Clearly, there was much work ahead of them. Right now, however, the cats needed rest. They hunted around for small animals and fished in creeks. They were sick and tired of the lousy corn bread the rats fed them. They needed more energy and good food.

"Humans and dogs can survive on plants but not cats," murmured a few hungry and skinny fishing cats. The others eagerly agreed.

After they had rested, Rascal said, "Goodbye fellows," and went with his friends back toward the Oregon Trail, where they had been not so long ago. Everything now seemed to be okay and things were returning to normal...but for how long?

"Look what I found," Lumby called out.

"What?" asked the others, their tails forming question marks.

"It's a hairball! A buffalo hairball! This is huge, not like mine! It's a round ball!"

"Calm down, Lumby, never gather others' belongings, you never know what may happen," the others cried.

Nervously looking around, Bunny added, "I think it was used by the native people for calling buffalo."

"I also found an unusual small reddish-brown rock the same size as the buffalo hairball and shaped something like a buffalo," said Lumby, happy and excited by his strange discovery.

Philosopher came closer to take a look, and then said, "The Blackfoot Indians had special mystic rites for calling buffalo herds close to their camp. The stone is called buffalo stone and was used to call buffalo to come close to be more easily hunted."

"Now we know who called the buffalo!" said Rascal.

"No, no, I was not calling them, I was just dancing and playing frisbee with the kittens," said Lumby.

The others seemed uncertain whether or not he was telling them a tall tale. They had no way of knowing for sure.

47

All day the cats searched for the Oregon Trail and by evening they found it. They were overjoyed when they ran into their friends, but then were very sad to discover that Sofia and the other cats were not there. Grey Dust was calling Onyx but there was no answer. Rascal hurriedly checked all the wagons but did not find the cats. Joking Horse was not there either. Something was definitely wrong.

Cynthia and Lou did not know where the cats went – they just were gone so fast that they did not know when and why. Everyone thought the cats had taken, as usual, their own paths. Besides, as they plodded along the endless gleaming roads, the pioneers' hearts were focused on their quest for a new home. They did not pay much (if any) attention to the cats, which was typical of human beings.

The empty, treeless plains, the endless horizon, the shimmering haze and thunderstorms bothered all of the travelers, animal and human alike. Everybody was tired of the hard times where mile after mile, day after day, the sun was hot, the wagons rolled up the long dusty road, the prickly pear grew in great abundance and nothing changed.

Grey Dust asked the others, "Why do you want to go to Oregon? There are lots of wild beasts, dry deserts, shifting sands and whirlwinds of dust there. The lands along the way are filled with cactus and prairie dogs everywhere. Oregon is rockbound, cheerless and uninviting. When I find Onyx I'll go east."

The cats decided to find a place to sleep somewhere on the prairie. They were concerned about Sofia, Onyx, Wandering Kitty and Number Seven. They ran straight…calling the names of their friends. Close to the Trail they found water barrels and a butter churn abandoned from former wagon trains. A little farther down they found a tar bucket and a chicken coop, an axe and a shovel. They imagined a coop full of clucking chickens raising a ruckus every time the wagon hit a rock and smiled to each other. They had a fun time imitating those chickens, forgetting for a moment about their lost friends.

They came to where the high barren prairie ended and stood and peered down the steep descent. Then as they stood on the heights they saw far away a few dark spots walking on the prairie.

"Sofia!" shouted Rascal.

"Onyx! Son!" Grey Dust's voice was shaking with happiness and he ran as fast as his four paws would take him.

As they got closer, they asked each other, "Is that

Sofia? Onyx? Wandering Kitty? Or just sage rabbits?"

Indeed, much to their consternation they soon realized that the animals they had spotted were not cats. They were three times the size of the common rabbit, white in color and slightly tinged with gray. They had short tails and long ears that were tipped with a darker color.

Grey Dust waved his paw in the air as a sign of friendship. He made the gesture and called to them as loudly as he could. He had not learned the language of sage rabbits well." As a result, instead of identifying him as a friendly cat, the sage rabbits cried, "Alien! Stranger! Danger!" They began backing off and hopped and ran away as fast as they could.

48

Meanwhile, traveling with another group of cats, Onyx caught sight of a golden eagle. He pointed to the sky and said, "Sofia, look! There's an eagle on his hunt."

Sofia, busy thinking about all the dangers and distraught at not being able to find her friends, asked mindlessly, "What's that?"

"It's a bird."

"So? No cat is afraid of a bird. A bird...an eagle... oh! Better run fast and hide somewhere," Sofia cried.

A little farther on, she spotted a colony of curious animals standing on their short hind legs and making sounds like a whistling barking noise. They were prairie dogs on guard and watching for danger.

They spotted the eagle and immediately sounded the alarm by stretching their heads into the sky and barking. Chirp-chirp-chirp! The call sent all of the prairie dogs into their burrows to hide. Onyx and Wandering Kitty dived for cover too, followed by Number Seven and Sofia. They had no choice, as a full panic had now set in.

The chirping soon stopped, however, as the little rodents slipped into their dark subterranean passageways. There the cats watched as, like family members, the rodents greeted each other with what looked like a kiss. They gently touched their front teeth together. It was not kissing though, it was simply the manner in which the prairie dogs recognized each other. These underground dwellers were about the size of rabbits. With their clay-colored coats with black-tipped hairs and a black-tipped tail and short legs with sharp claws, they looked strange to the cats. There seemed to be no end to the number and variety of strange creatures they had encountered out here in the wilderness.

49

The cats sat quietly, not wishing to kiss these peculiar animals. They did not know how these creatures would react if they discovered that there were strange cats in their burrows.

Sofia whispered to Wandering Kitty, "Are they dogs or squirrels?"

"Despite their doggy name, prairie dogs are members of the squirrel family," Wandering Kitty whispered back. "They dig a complex series of tunnels, called towns, deep into the ground. Hundreds of prairie dogs live together in towns."

"What do they eat? I'm hungry now."

"They feed on grasses, roots, leaves and flowers."

Suddenly Onyx jumped. "Somebody is calling my name!"

The cats sneaked out and saw a familiar group not too far away. The prairie dogs now emitted more pitched warning barks that signaled different types of predators. But this time it was a false alarm: the cats were friendly creatures. The watchdog arched his back making a jump followed by a shrill yip. This occurs when a predator has left the area, or the danger recedes.

Now the cats were hugging and telling about their adventures with joyful voices. Grey Dust was crying happy tears. "You are alive, my dear son, you are alive. Now let's free our mom." For sure, nobody was whispering anymore.

Together the cats went to say goodbye to the rest of the group. Frosty explained his hot desire to learn writing and reading. "Almost more than anything we wanted to be able to read and write, but rats punished us for trying to learn. Mighty curious, I looked at the rats' books, but couldn't touch them. Instead, I looked at how persistent the grass is and from it I learned persistence. From the trees I learned patience. Now I can go and learn how to write and read!" He was looking silently at the setting sun tinged with purple and gold, while tears rolled down his whiskers. But they were happy tears.

They said their final farewells and wished one another a nice trip. The former slave cats with Grey Dust and Onyx headed east and Rascal with all his friends went west, trying to catch the wagon train. Number Seven decided to stay to find Joking Horse. He missed his new friend badly, and he had no family in the East.

"Joking Horse! Where are you?" Number Seven was calling his friend in his mind. He imagined his face very vividly. So vividly that he saw every wrinkle, smelled his body, heard his voice and imagined those wise dark eyes were lurking everywhere in the grass.

"Don't worry, my friend, we will soon meet Joking Horse. I miss him, too. He's such a nice human and he knows lots of stuff," said Rascal, looking tenderly at his friend.

50

After many hours of travel, at last the cats saw some trees. "Let's go and make camp in the trees, then tomorrow we'll catch up with the Oregon wagon train," they said.

As they got closer it looked more like a forest than only a clump of trees. Among the beautiful pines the cats found themselves looking at a strangely curved tree. It was a white oak, much higher than a cat could stretch. The trunk of the tree took a 90 degrees turn to the right and it was parallel to the ground for the length of two relaxed cats and then again turned straight up. It looked like many years ago the sapling was bent and kept in a horizontal position until the first curve was fixed with growth and then a natural trend of the tree allowed it to grow upright and it straightened the upper part.

Just after noticing this tree, the cats looked up in all directions and it soon became very apparent that it was an old Indian trail. They looked for more bent trees and indeed found them. All the bent trees marked a very old, well-beaten path snaking its way to the ridge top. They were all quite impressed with this new discovery and eager to do more exploring.

Philosopher said, "I'm very curios to see this unexplored country. This place has never yet been visited by any cat."

The sun quickly sank behind the trees and then the darkness of nighttime fell. Soon the cats noticed the bright light of a campfire. Sneaking quietly, their paws barely making a sound, the cats crept up closer to discover that Joking Horse was seated near the fire.

"Nice to see you, Joking Horse!" said Rascal and gave him a hug.

"Thank you! Thanks, fellows!" said the human with a smile as he hugged and petted every cat.

Number Seven was in seventh heaven; he was purring and purring happy songs of friendship and love for humans.

"The fire smells nice and it's a wood fire," remarked Rascal.

Joking Horse smiled. "Yes, indeed, all the time across the prairies our fuel for cooking had been dried buffalo dung." After a longer pause, he added, "It's good you found me. It's dark now and we can't go anywhere, but tomorrow I'll need your help," he said in a mysterious voice and took out a strange, ugly looking eaglet. "This small creature fell down from the nest and I was having trouble putting it up in that very high tree"

"But it's no problem for me" said Rascal with a nod

of supreme confidence.

"Is the eaglet still alive?" asked Bunny.

"Yes," answered Joking Horse quietly.

After eating buffalo pemmican for supper, the cats went to sleep curled around the fire.

51

Morning dawned bright and fresh. There was no time to prepare a fire to make breakfast so they strode along the old Indian trail. Joking Horse went first and behind him the cats, with tails up, marched with braveness, curiosity and stamina. They arrived at a tall tree with one branch going up like a hand lifting. Above them a pair of eagles circled around in the clear blue sky as if looking for something, their high pitched squealing voices KEE-KEE-KEE sending shivers over the cats' backs, making their tails very bushy.

Under the tree Joking Horse took out his neck bandana and put the eaglet inside. He needed to know which cat could carry the baby to the nest. All of them wanted to do it. Finally it was decided that Rascal and Lumby were the best climbers. Rascal took the cloth into his mouth from one side and from the other side Lumby did the same and they started climbing up slowly and carefully.

The nest was made of large sticks containing aromatic leaves that served to deter insects. The eagle parents were so ecstatic that they gave Rascal a feather as gratitude and respect to all cats. Rascal looked at the huge birds with the golden feathers on the backs of their necks and their dark brown plumage. The parents walked with their talons balled into fists to avoid accidentally skewering the baby. Rascal and Lumby carefully climbed back down the tree.

Once they were on the ground again, Joking Horse explained what had just taken place. "An eagle feather given to somebody is the highest honor that can be awarded. The feather represents honesty, truth, strength, courage, wisdom, power and freedom."

Rascal told the group that the feather belonged to all the cats and he would like to share that honor with them. He would not carry on himself, as he did not want to boast (well, maybe he did want to, just a little, but he knew better).

"Now we go back to our Oregon wagon train," Joking Horse said as he pointed to the west. Then he looked up and saw the pair of eagles whirling through the air with their talons locked together. It was their dance of happiness.

"Yee-Haw! Yee-Haw!" Lumby was dancing his dance of the Wild West. All of them couldn't help but smile at the exuberant cute little kitten.

After a short time it began to rain lightly.

"At least the baby eaglet is safe now," remarked Rascal, looking worried about the coming rain.

"We have to wait for the storm to pass," advised Philosopher.

"Don't stand under the tree," said Joking Horse,

moving toward the opening. Then he knelt with his hands on the ground keeping his head low telling the cats that this was the best position to avoid being hit by lightning.

"When you see lightning, count the seconds until thunder is heard and divide by five," said Joking Horse, seeing how afraid the cats had become. "That will tell us how many miles the storm is from us."

"What happens if it's only a few seconds from when I see the flash and hear the boom?" asked Lumby.

But there was no time for an answer. A blinding flash lit up the sky, followed immediately by a strong boom that made them shiver. Terrified, they watched in horror as fire engulfed the branches on the huge tree where the eagles were nesting.

"We must help!" shouted Rascal.

"We must get a hand saw," cried Philosopher. "We can save them if we cut off the flaming branches."

They ran with Joking Horse, who said he had a saw, and arrived at the flaming tree just in time. Rascal bravely climbed up toward the burning branches and began sawing away with all his might. In less than a minute, the tree limbs fell to the ground, where the other cats stomped out the fire. The eagles' nest was saved!

52

After a few hours of walking on the prairie they found a place where a few days ago there had been a camp. But by now the wagons had already advanced several more miles down the trail.

"They'll be in Oregon already by the time we catch up with them," complained Sofia.

Joking Horse was paying no attention to her. He called for his horse, named Princess. Soon they saw the galloping horse approaching. The name most certainly did not match the horse's appearance. She was an old mare of a dirty white color.

"He should call her Ugliness," Dandy whispered to Snow.

"Beauty is only skin deep," remarked Rascal.

Dandy and Snow were embarrassed. They knew Rascal was right. Only a fool judges a book by its cover.

"Who is driving your wagon, Joking Horse"? asked Wandering Kitty.

"My cousin."

"You never told me that," exclaimed Number Seven in surprise.

"My cousin wants to be a screenplay writer and he's preparing a movie about the Wild West. That is why he's making this journey. Think what an exciting film it will make!"

"Will he write about cats too?" asked Rascal, thinking how wonderful it would be to be forever memorialized on the silver screen.

"Yep, it'll be a very interesting movie."

"How will we ride this horse?" asked Sofia, getting the stars out of their eyes and bringing them back down to earth and to the reality of their present situation.

"I saw a chicken coop nearby!" said Rascal with a big grin. As always, necessity proved to be the mother of invention.

Their improvised contraption worked well enough, even if its appearance was rather odd. It looked quite funny when Joking Horse took two chicken coops, with the cats inside, and fastened them onto both sides of his horse. But at least it meant that the cats were riding faster than they could walk. Otherwise they would never catch the wagon train (and Sofia's complaint would have been correct). The cats realized that they should never had made fun of the chickens in these wire cages, because now the tables were turned, and they were the ones inside! Life has a way sometimes of bringing about the strangest of ironies.

53

They traveled in the hot sun all day and did not catch up with the migrants yet.

"Please, Joking Horse, when will we be close to the wagons? Please, get us out from this wire cage before we get to camp. Otherwise all the dogs will call us chickens" pleaded Dandy.

"Okay," he agreed.

They noticed a lot of dust ahead of them.

"What's that?" asked Joking Horse, looking ahead.

"It's a stampede! Buffalo! Run!" shouted Rascal, and they hid behind the rocks.

As the stampede got closer, it looked, not like buffalo, but like cows, horses and mules from the Oregon wagon train running home towards the east.

"We have to turn them back, otherwise humans without animals will never make it to Oregon," said Rascal.

"How?" Someone asked.

"Let's make lots of noise," advised Joking Horse, jumping on his mare. All the cats made a huge ruckus, shouting and screaming, and helped to turn back the spooked animals. After a while all the animals turned back, except for two mules with packets on their backs. They just stood and would not move. What they say about mules being stubborn really is true.

They decided to take the two mules with them. Joking Horse helped the cats to jump on the mules' backs. The chicken coop was not needed anymore.

The day was bright and fair and every part of the journey looked pleasant, until the mules started with the most provoking tricks. The first mule, by well-performed jumping, juggled all the packets from his back to between his legs. When this was done, he scampered off gleefully. The other was following the trick but stopped and commenced kicking, pawing, floundering and bellowing.

Finally, everything went back to normal – the other mule came back and Joking Horse put all the packages in their proper order.

Joking Horse was riding his mare, in front of him sat Number Seven and Wandering Kitty who did not want to ride a mule.

Rascal, Philosopher, Bunny and Lumby were comfortably seated on the first mule. They named him Jackass Puzzle. Snow, Dandy and Sofia rode the other mule, which they named Old MacMule.

No matter how stubborn anyone is, the sun never changes its trek across the sky and night always follows day. With a small campfire and lots of food there was no worry about tomorrow. Before sleeping they talked about mules.

"At first, when I saw those two mules, I believed we'd have a nice, easy and luxurious trip, but I'm not delighted with the results of their cranky humors," said Wandering Kitty.

"It requires a lot of patience to manage packed mules," said Joking Horse. "They have other tricks too, like tossing their packs into a mud hole...and they are more accurate in placing a kick into you than a horse."

"I read stories that they very often go when they should stop and stop when they should be going," said Philosopher.

"Why are they so stubborn?" asked Lumby, his head cocked in curiosity.

"What you call stubbornness in a mule is his ability to think independently with lots of sense of self preservation. This is what makes them more reliable in hairy situations," explained Joking Horse.

"What do you mean by 'hairy situations'?" asked the kitten.

Rascal smiled and quickly answered, "It means those situations where all your hair stands up."

"I guess that most people aren't smart enough to be around mules. People say that mules are stubborn but they are just very smart and the point is to out-think them," said Joking Horse with a smile. Then he explained, "A mule is a cross between a male donkey and a female horse. By the way, you can tell a horse what to do and he will do it for you but with a mule you have to negotiate."

Lumby, in wide-eyed wonder, said, "A donkey and a horse? Wouldn't that make a Dorse?"

They all shared a warm-hearted laugh over his naivety.

The next day both mules were good and did no pranks. About noon, to everyone's surprise, they met an older man alone on the road. He was sitting and asking for food. Helping others is a great idea and Joking Horse and the cats gave the poor man everything he needed including blankets, food, and clothes. He was very grateful for all that he received – at least for now...

54

They traveled together now. The man said that he was lost and deserted by his friends. He rode the younger mule named Jackass Puzzle. Sofia was now riding with Rascal on the other mule. Snow and Dandy went on the horse with Joking Horse.

It turned out that the stranger was named Grumpy Uncle. He talked all the time, blaming everyone and everything all the way. He told them about bad Indians attacking migrant trains, killing everyone. So he advised them to stop for the night, make a fire, eat supper, and after dark pack the mules, saddle the horse and go for a few more miles, then sleep without a fire, quietly. Joking Horse did not believe in these attacks but in case some crazy troop was in the area he took the advice to heart.

That evening they still had not caught up with the Oregon wagon train. They had a nice supper and were enjoying the very pleasant weather. Then, after night-fall, they walked five more miles and went to sleep. Grumpy Uncle advised them to cover the white mare with a dark blanket so that Indians would not spot her.

The morning brought a surprise. Grumpy Uncle was missing and with him the horse and the mules and everything they had.

"He's a horse thief," groaned Rascal, ready to run after him.

"Take this," said Joking Horse, giving him a whistle. "When you see my mare, just whistle"

"OK," said Rascal, nodding, and was gone.

Lumby confessed that he saw the man taking the horse and mules but he thought he would be back with them. After that, explained the small kitten, he had fallen into a deep sleep. He had no way of knowing what was really happening, of course, and none of the cats blamed him for that. But now they had a major problem to deal with.

The thief knew that humans on foot could not catch a horse and was quietly riding away. When he spotted the orange cat not too far behind him he broke into a gallop. Rascal did what he was supposed to do – he whistled. The old mare knew what that meant. She stopped suddenly on the spot and Grumpy Uncle did a nice somersault over her head and landed with a painful cry on the hard, dry prairie. Rascal jumped onto the mare, the mules were roped to the saddle, so they followed the mare and they all galloped off leaving the man alone. The man could not go anywhere, as he was stuck in a prickly pear cactus.

Rascal guided Joking Horse with rest of the cats back to where he had left Grumpy Uncle, who was still lying in the cactus.

"Did nature give back to you, horse thief?" asked Joking Horse. "We should leave you here, like you did with us, leaving us alone on the prairie to die, but I'm not a bad guy and I'll take you to our camp and put you under the command of our captain…"

"I want to be a sheriff and deal with bad guys," said Wandering Kitty suddenly.

"You'll have enough work with rats, my friend," said Rascal, smiling with a mysterious gleam in his eyes.

"Let's go," Joking Horse commanded, and he put Grumpy Uncle across his horse and sat behind him to watch him carefully. The whole back of the thief looked like a porcupine.

They were riding to catch up with the pioneers. The doctor would help take out the painful needles in Grumpy's back. Soon they saw a serpentine of wagons. The mare and mules went into a fast trot, leaving a cloud of dust behind. Suddenly, the wagons stopped and were quickly forming a circle. All the animals and women with children stayed inside, but all the men with guns were hidden behind the wagons and ready to fire.

"Stop!" commanded Joking Horse. "They don't recognize us, they think Indians are attacking. One of you has to go to the camp and tell Cynthia that we are coming in peace."

Wandering Kitty said that it was his duty to do that. He got permission from Joking Horse and carefully made his way forward, well masked by the sandy color of the prairie. Soon everything was clear and everybody had lots of laughs. Only the thief was not too happy. Even though his back was soon rid of the cactus needles, he knew that in Fort Laramie a trial was waiting for him. The cactus needles were removed by using raw hoe-cake and waiting until the dough dried.

The cats learned what hoe-cake was. Mix a stiff dough corn or wheat flour with water and a little salt. Rub some buffalo lard on the hoe, and then heat it in the fire. Place the flattened cake on the hoe and hold until brown but not burned. Turn and brown the other side. It can also be baked in hot ashes or with hot stones. It's not the tastiest treat in the world, but it will surely fill your belly when it's empty after a long, hard day of traveling across the open prairie.

55

Two days later, near the junction of the North and South Platte, Rascal asked, "Why do we have to cross here?"

"If we stay on the south side of the river we'll reach a dead end somewhere to the south. So we have to cross the river to connect with the North Platte River," answered Wandering Kitty.

Here the people and cats encountered a very serious annoyance – black gnats.

"Just what is a gnat anyway?" the cats asked.

Cynthia explained, "Gnats are really flies but because of their small size and annoying behavior they just named them buffalo gnats, eye gnats, black gnats, or just plain old gnats. Since these pests tend to stay in territories, once you kill off the ones that are active around you, the others won't come too quickly. Their bites won't heal quickly either and when they fly into your mouth, ears, nose or eyes, they can bite there too!" Cynthia's face was swollen from the gnat bites and she could scarcely see. They ached like a toothache. Clearly, she was speaking from experience.

High up on the north fork of the Platte River,

the monotonous prairie landscape began to shift and change. A strange shape, rising up along the river, was the first landmark seen by pioneers heading west. The weary travelers greeted the change in landscape with enormous relief.

To everyone who had never seen a mountain, Courthouse Rock and Jailhouse Rock were a big surprise.

"Let's take a side trip just to get a closer look," said Rascal, always curious about new things.

Bunny noted, "That's the most curious formation I've ever seen."

Some called Courthouse Rock a 'castle' or 'solitary tower' and Joking Horse and nine cats went over to take a look at it. They climbed to the top and engraved their names on it as others had done. They spent about an hour on the summit writing. Then they became dizzy and it was time to go down to catch up with the wagons. The rest of the migrants were back on the trail and heading west again. Suddenly Joking Horse realized that they had left camp without a gun, pistol or knife, which was not a wise move because they were in a very dangerous area. There were said to be roving packs of ravenous wolves around, as well as perhaps an even greater hazard: bull snakes!

Not to be confused with rattlesnakes, these serpents sometimes grow to a length of seven feet. They are yellowish, with reddish-brown to black blotches on their backs; their bellies are usually cream colored, with brown or black blotches. They have a boldly patterned tail that is banded with black or dark brown and tan. Altogether, a very fearsome sight indeed.

Bull snakes may vibrate the tail when alarmed, which may sound like a rattlesnake (their cousins), but they also makes a hissing noise. These dastardly creatures usually seize prey with their mouth and, if the prey is large, wrap several coils around it and kill by constriction. All the more reason to want to avoid them!

These crafty snakes use their tongues to smell. The bull snake is quite the actor, putting on an impressive impersonation of a rattlesnake when threatened. It flattens its head, puffs up its body, shakes its tail, hisses loudly, and strikes repeatedly. It will hiss loudly or even posture itself in an S-shaped curve to deter potential threats – which works almost every single time.

Bunny was explaining to Lumby all he had learned about bull snakes. The young kitten thought it would be "cool" to meet such an exotic creature, but Bunny issued a stern warning: "Stay away from them. A little one such as you would make a tasty little snack for them."

After that, Lumby was not so eager to encounter a bull snake, but he was still eager to hear more about them.

Bunny continued, "They have a long, lithe body and a pointed tail. Rattlesnakes, by contrast, have a chunky body and a blunt tail with a rattle on the end. Bull snakes have a head and neck that are the same width. Rattlesnakes have a wide head and a narrow neck. Bull snakes have round pupils and rattlesnakes have pupils that are vertical slits. And of course, bull snakes do not have rattles and are not poisonous, while rattlesnakes do have rattles and are poisonous. Unfortunately, if bull snakes are cornered and frightened they will vibrate their tails and will strike and bite. If they are in dry grass, the noise that is made can be mistaken for the rattle of a rattlesnake."

56

The next day when they all woke up and were ready for some more travel, they suddenly heard a loud shriek. It was Sofia. "Great cats!" she wailed. "Lumby is gone!"

They searched all around the camp, figuring he was just playing one of his hiding games as he often liked to do. But he was nowhere to be found. This was no game. They quickly organized a search party and set off to find their little friend.

After two hours they were as befuddled as when they first began. "Where could he possibly be? asked Philosopher, perplexed. "We must think logically. If we were Lumby, where would we want to be."

Just then, Bunny, who had been quiet, spoke up. "Oh no! Me and my colorful stories about the bull snakes. He was so curious about what I told him I regret ever having said any of it." They resumed their search, and then an idea dawned on Bunny and he raised his front right paw into the air. "I think I know where he is! Follow me before it's too late!"

And off they went, to the very area where Bunny had told Lumby he might find bull snakes. "But I told him never to come here," Bunny lamented.

"Which is exactly why he would come here," said Rascal. "You know how curious kittens are. Why, I remember when I was little…"

Before he could say another word, as they rounded a bend they all beheld a dreadful sight: Lumby in the mouth of a bull snake! As the others gasped in horror, Rascal bravely rushed forward and pried apart the angry snake's powerful jaws. Bunny and Dandy then sprang into action and pulled Lumby's tail until they finally wrested the poor kitten free of the snake's grasp.

But they seemed to be too late. Lumby had stopped breathing! Sophia ran up to the lifeless kitten and pressed her mouth to his.

"What's she doing?" asked Dandy. "This is no time for kissing!"

"It's called mouth to mouth resuscitation," said Philosopher. "It will revive him"

And sure enough it did. After a few scary moments, Lumby began breathing again. It was a close call, but due to his friends' quick thinking, he was back to his usual playful self in no time.

57

Days followed days. The cats were not involved in any more adventures, so Rascal wrote about their trip in his diary, but he forgot to write which day it was.

*We saw elevated rocks...the first one was **Courthouse** and the smaller companion was **Jailhouse Rock**. Beyond those funny rocks, other greater wonders loomed up from the plain: **Chimney Rock,** which looks like a tall chimney. The enthusiastic cats tried to climb the massive rock but none got higher than the base. Chimney Rock is one of the most picturesque landmarks along the Oregon Trail. It signals the end of the prairies, as the trail becomes more steep and rugged heading west toward the Rocky Mountains. Then we came to **Scott's Bluff,** which is a large, steep, saddle-shaped cliff. Natives called it Me-a-pa-te, which means "The hill that is hard to go around." Having taken a good look at it myself, it is very clear to me why they came* up with that particular name. It is quite appropriate.

"We should be grateful that at least one-third of our journey is behind," said Wandering Kitty today. Dear Diary, for everyone who wants to know about bluffs:

(Geologically, the bluffs are composed of layers of siltstone and sandstone lying below layers of limestone and volcanic ash. The lower layers, being softer than the upper layers, are eroded by weather slightly each day...wind... rain... ice ...cause the rocks to be loosened and fall.)

Dear Diary, again on the road. We camped for a few days near Fort Laramie. The fort was begun by fur traders where the North Platte and Laramie rivers meet.

The first sign of civilization in six weeks! Hurrrra, Meowowow, Yodle-ay-eeee-hooooo!!!! It was a unique change from the endless wilderness. How beautiful it is to do nothing and then rest afterward!!!

Here we remained a few days, women from the trail washed clothes and the men went to the small town to buy anything they needed to repair the wagon, or some bacon and flour. But then the worst thing happened, worse than the hard hailstorm which hailed last night. Our friend Wandering Kitty left us. He went with his human family to California, looking for gold. We are going west to Oregon. Oh, meow, how I miss my home, my bed, my cat food. Some migrants just gave up the dream, turned around and went home back to the East. But most of them made the decision to push ahead no matter what. Our journey had three possible outcomes: the pioneers could either turn back and return to their former homes, make it all the way to Oregon, or die before winter hit.

The daily routine of breaking camp, walking, making camp again in the evening and eating the same food day after day was so boring. Lots of dust on the road.

When we passed **Independence Rock,** (I had thought that the President named it but I later found out that it was actually a pioneer), there we were chiseling messages to others following behind. It was fun and we left many scratch marks too.

Immediately after leaving Independence Rock we came in sight of the well-known **Devil's Gate.** With many others we paid this gate a visit. It is a narrow space where the Sweetwater River breaks through the Rattle Snake Mountain. I found it to be very much worth seeing. It was nature's art not the devil's work. We have still to go through South Pass to get through the Rocky Mountains. It is a dry, arid 20-mile wide gateway. After Soda Spring we *would be close to Oregon. At long last!*

What's the noise outside of the tent? For now, Dear Diary, I must check it out...

Mighty rascally Rascal.

Outside of the tent children were playing games they had invented during their travels. Rascal watched them with amusement in his eyes. One of their favorites was Shadow Tag, which was mostly for the smaller children: They needed a sunny day for this game, as it involved the children trying to step on each other's shadows.

Potato Race was another popular game. The kids placed potatoes in buckets at the starting line and worked in teams of two. Each child grabbed a potato from a bucket and ran eight feet to a marked spot, deposited the potato and then ran back for another one. He or she left it at a marked spot farther on and then further still. The child's partner ran to the first potato and brought it back to the bucket, then returned for another until all the potatoes were gathered.

The pioneer children also enjoyed racing "wheelbarrows," which went something like this. One kid picked up the ankles of another, who walked on his or her hands from the start to a marked spot some distance away. The contestants then changed places and raced back to the starting line

Another fun race was the Sack Race, in which each participant stepped into a burlap bag, purchased from a farm store, then hopped from the starting line to a line 40 feet away, then hopped back as fast as possible.

And finally there was the children's all-time favorite, the Three-Legged Race. They would stand side by side and fasten some sort of rope or cord between their two touching legs – in this way each team of two people had "three legs". They then ran and tumbled and stumbled their way to the finish line. Their playful laughter filled the air...

But even as he was enjoying the children's playing, Rascal's intuition told him that there was another noise too. Something that he needed to investigate. He went out of the camp, climbed to the top of a small hill and he saw a lonely horse galloping towards him. As it got closer he noticed that Wandering Kitty was sitting on its back.

"Please, Rascal, help me. Get all your friends, more horses are waiting for them, and let's go. The Oregon Trail can do without you. Let's help the cats that are stuck in the gold mine."

"What about Cynthia?" asked Rascal, concerned.

"Tell her we'll be back one day to visit her or we'll catch up on the trip farther up. Okay, for now, tell your friends and meet me at the gold mine. I'm counting on you to help me, my friend."

And with that, he was gone. Rascal knew exactly what he had to do. He could never say no when it came to helping out a friend.

58

The horseback cats arrived at the gold digging and panning area. The place was near South Pass, not too far from where the Oregon Trail would soon cross the Rocky Mountains. They circled around because they did not want be seen by the rats. Wandering Kitty led them to the forest. They got off the horses and let them graze, then followed him through the maze of stones and trees. They carefully looked towards the camp. The cats were furiously digging and panning for gold while the rats were resting under the trees.

Rascal, Philosopher and the rest sat hidden under a great pine tree. They had lots of time to decide what to do and how to help the digging cats. Wandering Kitty brought some food for them and told them what happened here.

"The kitties are free and they may go anytime but they want to get rich and so they are working hard. But the smart rats set up the camp and lead the cats. They don't dig, they sell equipment for a huge price. They even cook for the cats and help with washing their fur. The catch is that they ask for lots of gold for their services. Daily diggings go towards food and shelter, so the cats have to dig more and stand in the cold water to pan more gold. The more gold that is panned, the higher the rats raise their prices. It's a vicious circle for the prospecting cats and they are good kitties. They've left parents and wives and children to come here and they've promised to go back soon with lots of gold to buy catnip farms or mice farms.

"A few prospector cats were smart. They brought their own equipment with them and they didn't buy food from the rats, but hunted the forest mice by themselves. They even found a cat's grass nearby. The gold fever didn't get to them and whatever they dug they just said, 'Enough, brothers, let's go home.' As they said they would do and now they are happily united with their families. The rest stayed here wanting to become rich quickly and be the most prosperous cats in the world. While their families are waiting for them to come back, they work desperately to make more gold but even the tiny bit left from high prices set by the rats, they're spending on games."

"Computer games?" asked Lumby, thinking this could be fun.

But Bunny whispered to him, "They don't have computers, Lumby. They haven't been invented yet. Now be quiet."

Wandering Kitty explained, "The same games the children play. The kids have them for free, but the rats charge the adults lots of gold dust and gold nuggets for every game."

Lumby asked if he could see the kitty games and Wandering Kitty took them to another place, where the rats or the prospecting cats would not see them and where they did indeed find cats that were playing. It was called the Feather Game. Ten cats were sitting in a circle and keeping the small feather in the air by blowing up on it.

Another, larger group of 20 cats formed a line and then leaned over on their front paws and knees. The last cat leaped over the next one's back and then over all the others. He stopped and became the frog to be leapt over by the next one. This game was known as Leapfrog.

"What we can do for them?" asked Rascal.

59

The group decided to make a quiet camp near the gold mine and have a discussion about what to do next and how to help the cats. First they started to purr to warm up a little bit, then with relaxed minds, each one was thinking of the best rescue possibilities.

Suddenly Rascal jumped up. "Listen, a human baby is crying somewhere in the forest."

They all perked up their ears; it was definitely the voice of a human baby crying. They sniffed and tried to pick up its smell. It cried again a little. They moved softly through the woods.

Finally, they saw a small pup porcupine raise its quills and swing around, ready to slap...

"It's not a human baby!" exclaimed Sofia with relief. Soon the mother porcupine came and took her baby with her, shooting an unfriendly glance at the cats.

That evening the cats were discussing how to help the domestic cats stuck in the gold mine.

"Maybe purring will help," suggested Lumby.

"Oh, no," answered Wandering Kitty. "It might make the rats less nasty but it won't convince the cats to go home without gold. We must find something to take them out of this."

"I have an idea," Philosopher pointed out. "What about if we enlist the help of the porcupines?"

"How?" asked Dandy, not sounding very encouraged by the idea.

"And what can porcupines do?" added Bunny with an equally skeptical tone.

Philosopher looked for a moment at his friend without a tail and replied, "As you may know, the porcupines are very noisy. They can scare a bunch of catnips out of everyone not accustomed to their row."

"How can we convince them to help us?" asked Sofia, with a worried furrow between her eyes.

Philosopher pointed at Lumby. "He's a friendly cat and we can send him to the porcupines with Bunny, who is also very friendly."

"Okay, okay, we are all friendly cats," said Dandy.

Philosopher looked at him. "Oh, yes, but these two guys are the most friendly of all the cats in Catanada."

"Okay!" decided Wandering Kitty. "I'll lead them, these two, to the place where porcupines live. Meantime we should establish smoke signals, in case something unexpected happens to us or to you."

"Smoke signals like the Natives do?" asked Rascal.

"Yes, and I'll explain how they work so we don't get confused," said Wandering Kitty. "You must find a high and visible place for us, a place where we will be waiting for your signals. In this wild country this is the best and fastest way of communication. One of you will lay logs and make a fire. Now we must prearrange the signals, which spell out the messages. So you'll cover and open the fire in a certain way. There will be long or shorter breaks between the smoke going up."

All the cats listened with rapt attention; only Lumby was nodding off, as he was tired from so much walking. He only heard the last words that Wandering Kitty had said: "Let's sleep now and early in the morning the porcupine search party will go."

60

The next day, as soon as the sun rose over the horizon, Wandering Kitty took Bunny and Lumby and went on foot to the location of the porcupines. They walked for about two and a half hours when all of a sudden a strange noise scared them. Lumby jumped up into the highest tree, Wandering Kitty hid behind a huge rock and Bunny hid under the fern, trembling.

Grizzly, cougar, Big Foot! A band of angry rats! were the only thoughts that swirled through their worried minds at that moment.

Soon, however, they gratefully discovered that it was just friendly talk between two young porcupines. Lumby jumped back to the ground and the others left their hiding spots to approach the prickly animals with curiosity. The porcupines stopped talking and took defensive positions. They treat everyone as an enemy until proved otherwise. They turned their backs, with quills exposed, which means in their body language "Go away." The cats looked astonished. They did not yet know porcupines' body language, not even Wandering Kitty. The porcupines saw that their 'message' did not work, so they tried sounds. They shivered all over with lightly closed jaws making their lower and upper teeth clatter together. The sound was soft but really scary and they repeated it again and again.

"We are friends of porcupines," Wandering Kitty tried to tell them in sign language used by all prairie and forest animals. Just in time, too, because the porcupines were ready to take stronger actions, which meant fighting and striking them with their club-like spiky tails.

61

Finally the prickly animals understood that the cats were not a threat to them and they turned their heads toward the newcomers instead of their backs. They grunted softly, "Welcome to our prickly world and if you are not an enemy, let's go nibble on something green."

Lumby waved his tail in a friendly manner. "Lumby! Put that tail down! They'll think you want to fight them. In porcupine society that means anger," whispered Bunny.

Lumby stopped waving his tail, lowered it and made a friendly face.

The porcupines took a long look at the cats and smiled, saying that they should be their cousins because of the big whiskers natural to both kinds of animals.

"Hi! I'm Lumby, the friendliest cat on this side of the forest. We'd like to make friends with you," said the kitten.

The porcupines looked at him very pleased. They shook their quills and said, "We are the most beautiful and wise porcupines on this side of the Rocky Mountains."

Lumby smiled and purred softly. "Now let's dance the dance of new friendships."

Then he did three somersaults and started waving his tail but then quietly put it down remembering what that meant. The porcupines looked on in amazement at his performance and tried to do the same. Unfortunately, halfway through, they did not make a full turn in the air and landed on their backs and stuck their needles into the soft moss. Now they were upside down with all four paws in the air and did not know what to do next.

One porcupine said, "We may not be very good dancers but we have great wisdom and beauty. Now can you help us?"

"Can you switch off your needles?" asked Bunny.

"No, I'm upside down and stuck," replied the porcupine.

"Everything in my stomach is turned upside down, hurry up," said another porcupine. "The good earth upside down doesn't look so friendly."

Wandering Kitty looked and remarked, "We must return them safely to their proper position, but how?"

Bunny was first with an idea. "Back home in our house, I was reading some of Philosopher's books and I have an idea. What if we slide two sticks under each of them, push the sticks up and turn them back up?"

So the cats put sticks under each of them and pushed up. Their needles became unstuck from the ground and the prickly animals were back on their feet.

The porcupines invited the cats to their community. The cats followed them and soon they reached a place where more porcupines were having a meeting. When they spotted the cats, they got so noisy that leaves fell from the trees. Finally their leader gave a sign and everyone became quiet. He asked, "Who are they?"

"They helped us when we were in trouble," answered the first porcupine.

"They want to learn our wisdom," added the second.

"We need your help," purred Bunny.

"How can we help?" asked the leader, the biggest porcupine with a brown to gold colored coat. He showed his dark orange sharp teeth when he smiled. His long hairs and quills made him look bigger and heavier.

Finally, the porcupines learned about the rats and the cats in the gold mine and agreed to help and try to find a plan that would work the best for the highest good of all creatures and would not harm even the rats.

62

Wandering Kitty was still talking to the porcupines making the plans, while Bunny and Lumby went to a high spot to send a message to Rascal and his friends.

They carried sticks and small pieces of tree branches to the one place they found on the top of a hill where the trees were not blocking the view. They also found green fern branches to cover the fire and send the smoke in a certain manner of coded message. They made the fire in the way they had learned from Rascal, who in turn had learned it from Joking Horse.

Bunny cried, "Lumby, log on! Send the trail mail to them fast!"

Bunny thought that Lumby could remember the message and ran for more logs, while Lumby closed his eyes and tried to remember the code. But he had fallen asleep during Rascal's lecture last evening and he had no idea now how to send the message.

He also wondered whether there was enough RAM (logs) in place to send the mail...

"Log on! Log on!" shouted Bunny from down the hill.

"I'm logging, I'm waiting for a connection" purred Lumby loudly. "Okay, I remember now!" he exclaimed and started signaling www.CatsAreRascals.com.

Bunny did not look at the signals, he was still busy gathering wood, but Rascal and the rats in the mines saw the signal. The rats understood what CatsAreRascals meant, but they did not know what www.com was. A message that is not understandable usually translates as something full of fear of the unknown.

The rats began preparing themselves to fight a strange enemy under the name of **WWW** who they thought was coming to get them. In their minds they saw an animal bigger than Bigfoot, more dangerous than a grizzly bear and swifter than a cougar. The expression "Cats Are Rascals" caused them to imagine that some band of new cats was coming along with that strange animal named www.com.

Meantime Rascal, Philosopher, Dandy, Snow and Sofia were laughing about the mistake. "It's my website," said Rascal with a mischievous smile.

"Lumby must have forgotten the real message, which should be that 'help is near,'" added Snow.

"He's spent too much time on the computer back home, forgetting that t-mail (trail mail) is not e-mail (electronic mail)," agreed Philosopher, nodding his head.

63

Wandering Kitty came up with a plan that the porcupines would visit the camp at night and take every single ax, or pickaxe, and every other tool needed to dig for gold. The sweat on axe handles contains salt, which is the best thing to munch on for porcupines. It is a true treasure for them, more precious than gold.. So there would be no real fight, they would just take away the tools that were the product of so much unhappiness for the cats being abused by rats.

The rats ran away after the scary www.com message (WWW is coming!!!!!) It was very fortunate that rats can be such fearful creatures. Bullies have the upper hand, but are quite cowardly when they believe they might have to oppose a powerful foe.

The porcupines were happy having salty things to eat, but sadly, in all of their happy crunching and munching, they ate Rascal's diary too!

Rascal was in despair. "How can I rewrite it all?" he wailed.

"Well, Rascal, it's a big loss, but we'll tell you what each of us remembers and you can write it all down again," said Philosopher, Dandy and Snow simultaneously, doing their utmost to console him.

Bunny approached Rascal and said, "Rascal, dear friend, I've always dreamed of being a writer like you. I've never told anybody this, but I've been secretly writing my own diary. Here, I hid it so the porcupines wouldn't get it."

Rascal smiled a wide smile from ear to ear. "Bunny, you are the biggest cat even though you have no tail. You are my best friend."

64

After dinner it was time to go and catch up with the Oregon Trail yet again. Wandering Kitty brought the horses and they were ready to go when they discovered that Lumby was missing.

"Oh no, where is he off to now?" cried Sofia.

They all breathed a sigh of relief, though, when they quickly discovered the precocious kitten in the porcupines' camp. It seemed that the prickly little animals truly loved him and they gave him a makeover – porcupine style! They shaved his long hair and in the middle of the back they attached spikes. It took a lot of persuasion for the cats to make him finally say farewell to his new friends and head back to the trail with them.

Cynthia was very relieved seeing all the cats back together. She loved all of them and she could not bear the thought of any of them not being with her.

65

After two more months they *finally* arrived in Oregon. The humans were soon very busy building their homes, working the fields and sowing seeds, to make a real country and a real home.

One day Joking Horse came to Rascal. "You're going back to Catanada, right?"

"Yes, can you help us with that?" Rascal asked him.

"I never abandon my friends. Tonight all of you come to my tent and at 10pm we will go to our homes."

Rascal ran back to tell his friends. "I have good news. You've been complaining lately and asking how we can get back home. Well, I just talked with our friend Joking Horse and he promised to help us go immediately...tonight."

And at 10pm sharp, the cats went to meet with Joking Horse, who was sitting on a big cottonwood log.

"Sit on that log," he said and all the cats sat down. Number Seven was purring on his lap.

Wandering Kitty sat on the grass and looked at

everybody with both sadness and happiness at the same time.

"Thank you very much, friends, for everything you have done. I'll stay here. It's my dream to help all the innocent cats in the Wild West. My dream is to be a good sheriff and keep law and order on the WWW (Wildly Wild West). My place is not in the peaceful Catanada which you've told me about."

Joking Horse smiled. "Okay, Wandering Kitty, you will be the sheriff, the great one. Good luck!"

"Good luck, our friend!" said all the cats in unison, "and take care of this country. It's our future!"

Wandering Kitty waved his right paw and disappeared into the forest.

"Now, my friends, close your eyes, and see yourself in the Enchanted Forest in Catanada, where Prehistoric Cat Samuel is waiting for you to hear of your adventures," said Joking Horse.

The cats closed their eyes and waited, but nothing happened.

"Well," said Dandy, "it seems this isn't working."

The cats opened their eyes, but Joking Horse and Number Seven were gone. It was daytime in the Enchanted Forest, which they knew well from other trips. After a brief talk with Samuel, they ran back home.

Lumby said, "Okay, let's dance the Porcupine Friendship, Wild West Adventures, and Arrived Home Safe dances."

Bunny added, "And the Old Attic Dance."

After Lumby finished his three dances and a few somersaults, the cats ran toward their house. They knew the way already.

66

Home sweet home! Everywhere in the world is good but home is the best. After a warm welcome the cats were happy to rest.

Only Rascal was still in his drawer waiting for something so Philosopher went to him. "Why aren't you going to sleep, my good brother?" he asked.

"I must finish my diary, about our last adventures," Rascal answered.

"Okay, Rascal, if you have to," said Philosopher and went to his basket and fell asleep, while Rascal wrote:

We are happy to be home now and I would like to add that the Oregon wagon train which we were traveling with arrived at its destination without loss of any human lives. Even the two wagons full of sticks, not ordinary sticks, but fruit trees, arrived in good condition. Soon the migrants will have fresh apples, pears, cherries and settle down and live peaceful and happy lives. They were lucky that we joined their train as we brought them good luck.

Dear Diary, I will end my writing now and go take rest too. Besides, I'm now taking a vacation from all the writing and wild adventures for sure. For some time I will not move from my home; I will stay here and lead a rather boring life full of catnip, good food, fresh water and lots of sleep. Sometimes I will add more pictures to my website www.CatsAreRascals.com. I might also write letters to the kids that send me their emails to Rascal@CatsAreRascals.com …

Mighty rascally Rascal ☺

Book 4 coming soon

About the Author

Boszenna Nowiki lives in Vancouver, Canada with her husband – captain of the seas – Pawell, and eight cats. "My cats came either from SPCA shelters, wondered over to my house as 'homeless cats', or they have been rescued from some abusive relationships," Boszenna says with a smile. *"I love what I do and I do what I love,"* she adds – that is taking care of her cats and promoting good moral values among children.

Boszenna does a great job in educating children about history, geography, zoology, survival skills and such positive moral values as friendship, loyalty, love, and trust, while at the same time filling her stories with fast action, magic and adventure. In her books Boszenna strives to provide for children and their families the best option to counterbalance the ever-present negativity, hatred and violence that children encounter in their everyday lives, especially on TV and in electronic games.

Why Some Cats Are Rascals

Book 1

Part 1: Quest for Freedom

Rascal the Cat and his companions are looking for freedom. Will they find it? Will they be able to get back home safely?

Part 2: Enchanted Forest

Enchanted Forest is very dangerous. There are many stories of cats that wandered into this forbidden place never to come back...but nothing can stop Rascal the Cat from having a mysterious and wild adventure. Not even the huge Prehistoric Mouse Tram-bam-bu! Will she change everyone to look like a mouse, eat like a mouse and even smell like a mouse?

Here is What the Readers Are Saying:

"You don't have to be a feline fancier to thoroughly enjoy the adventures of Rascal and his pals as they venture into the great world seeking freedom. You see, Grandma Cat has whetted their appetite for seeing more than their comfortable home with her stories of when she was young: '... her tall tales of sleeping in the rubbish can and under the stars and about the fancy Ball that the cats used to organize two times a year.'"

—Gail Cooke, Top 4 Amazon.com reviewer

Look for this book in your local library or your local bookstore.
Get it directly from the publisher by calling toll-free 1–888–575 3173 or by visiting the publisher's website www.StartHealthyLife.com

Why Some Cats Are Rascals

Book 2

The second book of the series begins with Rascal and his feline companions arriving in the Sahara desert at the time of the pharaohs – a dream place for cats, as their significance and social status rises to that of semi-gods. However Rascal and his gang do not entirely fit the established way of life and the belief systems of ancient Egypt and they have to run back to Catanada to escape being sacrificed at the altar of Egyptian god.

Before they arrive back home to defend it from a gang of thieves, they first have to travel through medieval Europe where they encounter misunderstandings, hatred and witch-hunts in all possible shapes and forms…

Here is What the Readers Are Saying:

"The two historical tales swish your attention like a cat's tail through constant action and learning. I was astonished to see how much educational information the author was able to impart without being preachy or talking down to young readers. Ancient Egypt looks into the veneration of cats, unusual animals and insects, the problems with rodents around the Pharaoh's granaries and superstitious beliefs about cats. The Medieval tale addresses the Black Death, politics at court and superstitious beliefs while adding its own unusual animal.

The final story about the "cat-foiled burglars" is pure humor. If my daughter had read this book at age 8, the house would have been filled with gales of laughter."

—Donald Mitchell, Top 3 Amazon.com reviewer

Look for this book in your local library or your local bookstore.
Get it directly from the publisher by calling toll-free 1–888–575 3173 or by visiting the publisher's website www.StartHealthyLife.com

Get all three Rascal adventure books for the price of two

Why Some Cats Are Rascals, Book 1...............US $8.95
Why Some Cats Are Rascals, Book 2...............US $9.95
Why Some Cats Are Rascals, Book 3................ Free

Subtotal	$18.90
Delivery	3.95
Total	$22.85

Send this page with your check or money order payable to **Healthy Life Press Inc.** to the following address:

Healthy Life Press Inc.
1685 H Street, PMB 860
Blaine, WA 98230
USA

Visit the publisher's website **www.StartHealthyLife.com** for more savings options.